To my Sister Jane — Thanks for all the wisdom you bring to my life.

Kit or Brother Kit

2016

Well Versed

Columbia Chapter
of the
Missouri Writers' Guild

Well Versed 2016

Copyright © 2016 by Columbia Chapter of the Missouri Writers' Guild
Managing Editor Liz Schulte
Cover design by The Cover Counts

All rights reserved.
Without limiting the rights under copyright reserved above, no part of this publication may be reproduced, stored in or introduced into a retrieval system, or transmitted, in any form, or by any means (electronic, mechanical, photocopying, recording, or otherwise) without the prior written permission of the Columbia Chapter of the Missouri Writers' Guild.

This is a work of fiction. Names, characters, places, brands, media, and incidents are either the product of the author's imagination or are used fictitiously. The Columbia Chapter of the Missouri Writers' Guild acknowledges the trademarked status and trademark owners of various products referenced in this work of fiction, which have been used without permission. The publication/use of these trademarks is not authorized, associated with, or sponsored by the trademark owners.

This eBook is licensed for your personal enjoyment only. This eBook may not be re-sold or given away to other people. If you would like to share this book with another person, please purchase an additional copy for each recipient. If you're reading this book and did not purchase it, or it was not purchased for your use only, then please return to your favorite eBook retailer and purchase your own copy. Thank you for respecting the hard work of our authorship.

Table of Contents

Well Versed Sponsors 1
Forward by President.. 2
Preface by Editor 3

Nonfiction 2016... 4
   Southern Icestorm by Lori Younker.. 5
   The Stranger by Sheree Nielsen 9
   My Season of Shoes by Pat Wahler 12
   He That Does Not Work Neither Shall He Eat! by Mary Rechenberg 15
   The Gift by C.A. Simonson 19
   Thumb and Forefinger by James Coffman 21
   Would A Thong Have Gone So Wrong? by Lynn Strand McIntosh ... 23

Fiction 2016 25
   Cellar Dweller by Frank Montagnino 26
   Spider Bite by Susannah Albert-Chandhok 31
   Secrets of a Shapeshifter by Laura Seabaugh 35
   A Telling Moment in a Changing Life by Kit Salter 40
   Audition by Susannah Albert-Chandhok 45
   Behind the Wire by Hope Longview 48
   Burned by Billie Holladay Skelley 54
   Chokehold by Diane Siracusa... 58
   Flight in Moonlight by Susan Koenig 63
   Fun on Wall Street by Von Pittman 70
   Goodwill by Andrea Lawless 76
   Hanging by a Thread by Maril Crabtree 79
   The Incident at Bleeding Creek Trestle by Pablo Baum 82
   Inescapable by Nancy Jo Cegla 87
   Secrets to a Dead Man by Brianna Boes 92
   To Be Cold by Karen Mocker Dabson... 97
   Unlocking the Past by Debra Sutton 99
   Wild Love by Rexanna Ipock-Brown.. 101

Poetry 2016 105

A Brief Encounter by Terry Allen 106
Night, Mid-February by Terry Allen 108
Horror by Peg Crawford..109
Mr. Snapper Flapper by Larry Allen 110
A Box of Old Pictures by James Coffman..111
A Fly by James Coffman..112
A Visit to Grandma's House by Eva Ridenour..113
All Day the Media by James Coffman 115
Alone on Stage by Billie Holladay Skelley 116
Black Cat by Sheree Nielsen..117
Campfire by Kayla Nilges 119
Catalpas by Eva Ridenour 120
Cave Man by Lee Ann Russell 121
Chains by C.A. Simonson...124
Choroidal Nevus by Nancy Jo Cegla 126
Circumvent by Kayla Nilges 129
The Corner Café by Nancy Jo Cegla 130
The Crows by Peg Crawford..133
Dark Lullaby by Laura Seabaugh 134
Elfin Heart by James Coffman..135
Evidence of a Still Life by Peg Crawford 137
Free Pain Evaluation for You or Your Horse by Terry Allen 139
Headstone Hopping by James Coffman...141
Here There Be Dragons by Peg Crawford 142
In The Garden by Maril Crabtree...143
Key Exchange by Danyele Read 144
Kill Your Darlings by Peg Crawford...145
The Last Crossing by Terry Allen..146
The Last Purr by Susan Koenig 149
The Light by C.A. Simonson..150
Measures to Destiny by Jessica Faulkner 151
The Mole Man by Larry Allen 152
Night Train by Eva Ridenour..153
The Oak-Branch Cross by Pablo Baum 154
Oh Venerable Lock by Ida Bettis Fogle 157
Out of the Mouth of Babes by Nancy Jo Cegla 158
Poetic License by Lee Ann Russell..161
Rat Snake by Terry Allen...162
Red Poppies by Nancy Jo Cegla 164
Remembrance by Barry Walker 166
Sequel by Lee Ann Russell 168
She Fell in Love by Larry Allen...169

Sherbet and Sweet, Crushed Macaroons by Nancy Jo Cegla 171
Thoughts After Touring the Former Missouri Penitentiary
    by Ida Bettis Fogle 173
Tonya Harding Counsels Lizzie Borden by Larry Allen 174
Too Pretty by Larry Allen 175
Trapped by C.A. Simonson 176
Treasures by Barbara Backes 178
Vacant Save For This by Kayla Nilges 179
Waiting by Hope Longview 180
Your Favorite Time of Year by Debra Sutton 181

Flash Fiction 183
    Maybe Next Time by Billie Holladay Skelley 184
    Heaven's Gate by Karen Mocker Dabson 185
    You'll Get a Charge Out of This by Frank Montagnino 186
    Other Lifetimes by Karen Mocker Dabson 187
    Secrets Unlocked by Amy Christianson 188
    The Secret of Life by Susannah Albert-Chandhok 189
    The Inheritance by Chinwe I. Ndubuka 190
    The Prince by Danyele Read 191
    The Wedding Dress by Amanda Booloodian 192
    Treasure in the Trunk by C.A. Simonson 193
    Wisconsin Cows by Amy Christianson 194
    Do Not Disturb by Hope Longview 195
    Backwards and in High Heels by Susan Koenig 196
    Life with Mother by Lori Younker 197
    The Queue by Julie Pimblett 198
    Out of Time by Rexanna Ipock-Brown 199
    Twisted Together by Hope Longview 200
    Research in Seattle by Liz Davis 201
    A Relative Quote by Carrie Koepke 202
    It's All Relative by Julie Pimblett 203
    It's All Relative by Debra Sutton 204
    I Bless the Rains by Hope Longview 205
    Untitled by Kathy Kelley 207
    Memories by Debra Kaye Sutton 208

Flash Fiction Time Capsule Contest 209

Appendices 218
    Appendix A: Contributors 218
    Appendix B: Columbia Chapter of the Missouri Writer's Guild 230

Appendix C: Well Versed Sponsors 231
Appendix D: Well Versed Judges 232

Well Versed Sponsors

Thank you to everyone who volunteered and financially contributed to this year's Well Versed. We could not have made this book without you.

Forward by President

May this edition of Well Versed truly divulge the heart and talents of our local collection of writers who call themselves the Columbia Writers Guild.

We network together at monthly meetings, critique one another's work, share the journey toward professional writing careers, and nurture new writers. Each time we meet we deepen our relationships with one another. Above all, our yearly publication bonds us together for posterity. It's all here, no longer under lock and key. Friendship opened the door.

Lori L. Younker, 2016 President

Preface by Editor

Once again it was another terrific year for submissions to the Well Versed anthology. Between these pages there are beautifully written poems, evocative flash fiction, inspiring nonfiction, and engrossing works of fiction. It has been a pleasure working with the talented individuals of the Columbia Chapter of the Missouri Writer's Guild.

Some of the work you read will fall within a theme of under lock and key. The phrase "under lock and key" generates ideas of secrets, heartbreak, unspoken feelings, little known stories of the past, hidden jewels, treasures in the attic, ghost stories, or mysteries to me, but the individuals who chose to write within the theme might have their own interpretation of the idea. The theme wasn't meant to confine, but to inspire writers to reach into themselves and find a story they didn't know was waiting to come out.

As you read further, I hope you enjoy the variety of subjects and narrative voices pulled together in this collection of work. The authors are from a wide array of ages, professional experience, and backgrounds. Together we hope to offer a terrific sample of the talent that lies in our vibrant community.

Liz Schulte, Editor

Photo by Nancy Jo Cegla

Nonfiction
2016

Southern Icestorm
by Lori Younker

First Place

Rain beat against our 1985 VW Quantum. I rested in the capable hands of my husband, Bill who never complained of fatigue nor ever fell asleep. With eyes on the road, both hands on the wheel, his Army training left no room for the concept of personal discomfort.

"What are you thinking about?" I asked when an hour of silence passed between us.

"Oh, nothing really," he replied.

"How much farther?"

"Three more hours to go."

I turned my head to the window, tucked my jacket under the crook in my neck, and let the side of my head rest against the cold glass. I slept.

Our plan to drive through the night meant that our three children could sleep away most of the trip from Chicago to Arkansas. We were off to see my step-grandmother to show off our newest addition, Mary, who was strapped in her car seat with blankets tucked around her shoulders.

Her sister Joanna, usually so alert and full of opinions, snoozed in the middle. Behind Bill, our carefree oldest, Peter, stared out the window wide awake, proudly wearing his new, blue winter coat which I had sewn for him. Those were the days before China provided all manner of household goods and clothing for the American masses. If we wanted something cheap we had to make it ourselves.

When sheets of ice whipped wildly against my window, I woke up with a start. Our little vehicle was taking a beating as it slid down the highway. The wind seemed to invade the interior of our car to with a pervasive, damp cold. Though the children were still sleeping soundly, I shivered with the strangeness of it all.

"Would you turn up the heat?" I asked, rubbing my hands

together.

"It's turned up as far as it will go."

I squinted at the clock on the dashboard, well after midnight and black as pitch on all sides. The only light to be seen was from our headlights which struggled to illuminate the road. I tried to locate the white stripe of paint that should skirt the edge of the highway.

"Where are we?" I asked.

"We already passed through Springfield. We turned off 44, and we're headed south on Highway 60." Bill replied, turning the windshield wipers to their highest speed.

The heater fan hummed, the wipers clicked back and forth. Indeed, we were on a two-lane highway that descended in large sweeping curves through dense forest.

"We've never been this way before," I said because I knew Bill was thinking it.

"Looks to me that the weatherman was wrong—there's ice."

"In all my years living in Upper Michigan, we never had an ice storm. I didn't even know there *was* such a thing," I said soberly.

The car's narrow wheels struggled to grip the road, and I shot a stern look at my husband.

Now fully awake, I watched the wiper blades push ice clumps back and forth, and they were getting larger by the moment.

"The defroster can't keep up," Bill said.

"Don't you think we should stop the car so we can clean off the wipers?"

There was no answer. Soldiers don't stop to clean off wipers.

All of a sudden, a thick blast of steam rose from the engine, and Bill put on the brakes, bringing our car to a slippery stop on the frosty. white shoulder of the road.

From the back seat, a little voice added more reality to our situation, "What happened?" Peter asked.

"Shh-hh, dear. Dad's checking the engine," I tried to sound reassuring.

Bill returned from the front of the car and got back in the driver's seat. "We've blown a radiator hose."

"What'll we do?" I asked.

"We should pray to Jesus," Peter announced.

The little children shall lead them. Isn't that what they say?

Just a few short months before, Peter and Joanna had survived a car accident, when the Ford Bronco their grandfather was driving was T-boned, spun out of control, flipped over, and was stopped by the light pole. "We were hanging upside down like monkeys," Joanna loved to report. "God kept us safe," said Peter.

Bill prayed aloud, and we waited in the dark, quiet car which quickly glazed with ice.

Not a single car passed in either direction.

My heart beat in my chest with the anxiety that a mother bear might have over the safety of her cubs. The temperature inside our vehicle plummeted with each passing second, and I held back the urge to say anything that would make things worse.

Less than five minutes passed when a set of large, brilliant headlights stopped behind our vehicle, and a bearded, middle-aged man in jeans and Army jacket met Bill in the sleeting rain. Over my shoulder I watched their silhouettes converse animatedly against the pick-up's bright beams. The light seemed to magnify the crystals of the freezing rain so that they shown like diamonds on black velvet.

Bill leaned back into the car with the news, "He says he'll take us to his shop in his truck to look for the part we need."

Amazed, I woke the girls. Pete and Joanna sat on a pile of oil rags in the back, and the three adults and a baby squeezed into the front.

The man leaned forward and smiled in my direction, "You ain't used to southern ice storms, are you?"

The wind and rain continued to beat down on us as we dashed from the pickup to a humble, one- pump gas station hiding in the woods. There was no time to think about how the station could thrive so far from the highway.

The man's wife welcomed us into the small building with solemn eyes. Joanna explored the three aisles lined with motor oil and packages of spark plugs.

"I was just about to turn in for the night," the wife said. "But y'all are cold and wet, so I'll make you up some hot chocolate."

Peter and Joanna enjoyed their middle of the night adventure. We sat at a wooden table with mugs of hot cocoa and plenty of giggles. Mary slept through it all.

The clock on the wall clicked passed two in the morning, when the door jingled to announce that the men had returned pleased they had found the part we needed at a friend's garage just a few miles down the road. We wouldn't be stranded for the night.

The man promptly delivered us to our car, to chip away at the ice and through trial and error, and Bill coaxed the length of radiator hose into place.

Cold and wet, we commenced through the darkness in a type of sacred silence, anxious for the heater fan to overtake the cold.

"I'm afraid we didn't say thank you," I whispered to Bill.

"Don't worry I did. Several times even."

What a selfless couple! Their service to us had no audience but our family of five. The middle-of-the-night rescue was a divine mystery. I felt a milky sleep pulling at my eyes. Perhaps it never happened at all. I turned my body to look at my dear children in the back seat, and the proof was there: cocoa spilled down the front of Peter's coat and Joanna's chocolate mustache.

The Stranger
by Sheree Nielsen

Second Place

As I sat quietly on the staircase landing, I peered from louvered windows into the darkness, and detected footsteps in the narrow breezeway between our home and the neighbors. The footsteps traveled in the direction of the wooden gate leading to our back yard. A slight aroma of cherry blended with figgy tobacco filled the breezeway.

Mom smelled the smoke wafting in through the louvered windows and asked, "Did you lock the basement door when you came in from playing?"

"Mom, I wasn't in the basement. I used the kitchen door to go in and out."

Frantically, Mom rushed the door in the center of house separating first floor from sub level. Turning the black skeleton key in the ornate keyhole cover, she locked and secured the heavy wooden door. To keep out the evil, I thought.

Dad worked second shift at the foundry, which was never easy for Mom. These were the nights she worried. These were sleepless nights for Mom.

The weathered pine screen door from the basement walk-out slammed hard, jarring my intuition and imagination. The cherry tobacco scent filled the basement.

I pictured a man in his forties, wearing a tailored dapple grey suit and felt fedora, and Tom McMahon leather shoes with waxy stiff shoelaces, and metal taps on the soles. He walked with confidence, yet daunting mystery.

The stranger, it seems, stopped and started. I heard the pause in his footsteps followed by a hint of fruity odor, as he puffed on what smelled like a cigar.

Wringing her hands, beads of sweat trickled from Mom's forehead onto a tousled lock of auburn hair past her perfectly rouged pink cheeks. I felt goosebumps rise on my arms. We were both terrified.

Her long graceful fingers quietly lifted the black rotary phone to dial, but another party was using the line.

Mom interrupted the conversation by whispering "Emergency, Emergency".

The other party hung up and she reset the phone by holding down the receiver. When she lifted it again, she heard the low obnoxious 'aaauuuu' of the dial tone. She whisked her index finger completely around the dial enabling the click, click, click nine times; followed by a short click of one, and then one again.

"There's an intruder in our basement. Please hurry!"

We peered through the beige sheers of our entry hall window until a police officer in a navy blue uniform with shiny silver buttons, and hard-brimmed hat appeared on our well-lit front porch.

Mom opened the door for the officer, who'd apparently already been informed of the intruder by his dispatcher.

"Stay here," said the man with chiseled jaw, sporting a toothy smile. He walked, flashlight in hand, and gun in holster, exiting through the kitchen onto our covered porch, and proceeded to the basement walk-out.

The basement, an unfinished open space, except for the coal room, housed black squares of coal for the furnace that sooted everything it touched.

We heard the quick gait of the officer, accompanied by the slight scent of Old Spice cologne. A knock on the door at the top of the stairs linking basement to kitchen, yielded an "all clear" by the man in blue. This prompted Mom to turn the skeleton key opening the door, releasing all evil spirits.

"I locked your basement door for you. Everything should be okay now."

"Thanks, Officer."

The officer stepped lightly as he tackled the steep fifteen steps to the sidewalk on Meramec Street.

Mom kicked off her black leather heels, and slipped on some fuzzy pink slippers, a jersey nightgown, and chenille robe. I gazed at her in amazement as she prepared a homemade concoction of whole milk, sugar, and Dutch cocoa in a two quart pan on the stove. The bluish yellow gas flame danced upward heating the cookpot's copper bottom.

I curled up in Dad's easy chair with a mug of her tasty beverage, and sipped the best hot chocolate this side of the Mississippi. Across from me, Mom rested on the couch – feet propped up on Dad's handmade mosaic table, with Family Circle magazine in hand. She flipped the pages until her eyes closed, losing grip of the magazine, and dropping it to the hardwood floor. I kissed her cheek, and covered her with a knit afghan.

I tip toed up the winding mahogany staircase, and plopped myself into the comfort of my twin-size bed. Strangers in the basement, hmm… Enough excitement for a young girl for one night! I hiked Grandma's floral-embroidered cotton quilt up high over my shoulders, allowing a few locks of my strawberry blonde hair to peek out from the covers.

I was awakened from slumber when the front door creaked open and shut. The sound of metal brushed glass – Dad setting his black lunch box on the entry way coffee table.

In the stillness of the night, I heard Dad say to Mom, "Honey, how was your evening?"

My Season of Shoes
by Pat Wahler

Third Place

Cleaning out my closet did more than organize me. It brought me face to face with a stunning reality. Apparently, I'm teetering on the brink of becoming a shoe hoarder. Shoved toward the farthest edges of the closet, my shoes brazenly tangle around each other like mismatched lovers. Not even I realized how many pairs I owned. I dropped the idea of shopping at an upcoming sale. Until I sorted through the suede, leather, and canvas on the floor, any new purchase would have to wait.

My nose wrinkled at the faintly musty aroma of old sneakers while I pulled out each secret treasure one by one. I found tan pumps I'd worn to a job interview next to sandals that traveled with me on a cruise to the Virgin Islands. There were the gray shoes worn to my mother's funeral and at the bottom of the pile, a pair of strappy silver sandals I wore to my daughter's wedding. That's when it occurred to me that in many ways my life could be chronicled by the shoes I've kept in my closet.

During teenage years, I read fashion magazines and worked hard to emulate the style of tall willowy British models. My skirts were as short as my mother and common decency would allow, but it took a sassy pair of brown leather knee-high boots to make me look totally groovy. The gleam in my boyfriend's eyes made the purchase worth every penny.

A few years later my boyfriend became my husband, and fashion magazines were replaced by television programs. Situation comedies showed me what it took to be a perfect mom. Since sexy was no longer in my job description, I transformed my wardrobe to a practical one. I needed clothes made of washable fabrics that resisted stains from wet burps and leaky diapers. My knee-high boots were pushed aside for scuffed penny loafers that helped me execute quick sprints after a wandering toddler without crossing over the dreaded line to matronly attire.

As the children got older, my ensemble required yet another makeover. I had a new career that called for sensible slacks, slinky long jackets, and a silk scarf tied in a bow around my neck. In those days, I wouldn't dream of being seen in a frilly dress and high heels because everyone knew the business world belonged to men. My unisex style brought a multitude of flat shoes in a palette of colors that sedately lined the closet floor. Their perfect uniformity generated a tiny issue. With eyes puffy from washing loads of late night laundry, I left for work wearing one navy shoe and one black. Donating the navy pair to a thrift shop prevented further trouble.

The years continued to streak past in what seemed like the blink of an eye. How did it happen that my children grew into adults so quickly? They began to carve out their own path in the working world as I found myself counting down months to retirement. Demands on my time dropped and so did workplace dress codes. I had the freedom to wear whatever I wanted, and what I wanted most was to feel good.

My personal style became what I now charitably refer to as non-business casual. When sidewalks sizzle, you can actually hear me coming. The slap-slap sound of my flip flops reminds me of a day at the beach rather than the reality of pushing a shopping cart. The north wind whistles, and I snuggle into sweatpants that stretch enough to bend when I do. Thick socks and walking shoes guaranteed to keep my feet stable are my favorite cold weather choice. I may look like I'm heading for the gym, but I never do.

I guess you could say from the very first time my mother laced a pair of sturdy white leather walkers on my feet, shoes have helped me get where I want to go. They've played a role in every joy and sorrow of my life. Whether walking a well-worn path or blazing a trail toward a brand new destination, shoes have done more than cover my feet. They've boosted my confidence, embellished my appearance, and always kept me standing tall. As my shoes evolved over the years, so did I. Time has a way of smoothing and polishing even the sharpest edges. I've become more soft and flexible, more relaxed and forgiving.

I can't help but wonder about what may come next in my season of shoes. After retirement, who knows? If 60 is the new 40, then there's still plenty of time to have a few more adventures before I slide into pink fuzzy house slippers. Come to think of it, I could even turn back the clock and become "sole" mates once again with a pair of brown leather knee-high boots. I predict such a move might even resurrect an oddly familiar gleam in my husband's eyes. There's only one thing I need to find out. Will my arch supports fit in sassy boots?

He That Does Not Work Neither Shall He Eat!

by Mary Rechenberg

If you ask a kid these days where their food comes from you may hear responses such as: "From the store" or "From a restaurant." That was not the case when I was growing up in the 1940's, 50's, and 60's. My sisters and I knew exactly where our food came from, having had a hand in the production, harvest, preparation, and preservation of the food our family consumed.

My parents, Joe and Ruby Kranawetter, my three sisters, Nancy, Kay, and Carol, and I lived on a farm in Cape Girardeau County, Missouri. We raised chickens, cattle, hogs, and at one time rabbits that provided meat for our table. We were all expected to help feed and water these animals, gather the eggs, tend the animals when they were sick, and run after them when they escaped from their pen.

We had milk cows that provided plenty of milk and cream. We sold most of the cream to the local dairy. A truck would come and pick up the big metal cream cans that we stored in the cellar. A cream separator sat in the corner of our farm kitchen. This apparatus had a large metal bowl on top where you poured the fresh milk. As the milk trickled down through the machine it somehow separated the cream from the skim milk. Two spouts at the bottom, one for the cream and one for the milk, guided the liquid into a bucket or jar just below each spout. This wonderful invention ran by muscle power (a hand crank) until Daddy could afford one powered by electricity.

Mama used the skim milk to make cottage cheese. Since we had more milk than we could drink, Daddy used milk mixed with ground feed to slop the hogs. We churned our own butter using some of the sweet rich cream.

I did not consider milking the cows my favorite chore as I had a great deal of trouble getting the milk to come out, no matter how hard I squeezed. At the young age of ten or eleven, balancing on the little stool that Daddy had made proved difficult. The cow switched her tail in my face and tried to put her foot forward—sometimes landing it in my bucket or knocking it over. I'm sure the cow felt annoyed by such an inexperienced milker.

I could handle gathering the eggs pretty well, and eggs played a big part in our diet. We had eggs for breakfast every morning. Eggs even provided part of our income as we raised several hundred chickens and sold hatching eggs. Reaching into the nest to pick up the eggs could sometimes be dangerous if a hen remained on the nest. Once I found a black snake in a nest, which almost turned me against gathering eggs. Life on the farm was a real adventure.

When the hens got older and a new batch of chickens were ready to move into the hen house, we had chicken butchering days. Mama didn't butcher just one chicken at a time. Even for a family dinner or company we butchered at least three or four, but on the big butchering days we worked on as many as ten or twenty.

Gallons of boiling water heated in a large black kettle over an open fire stood ready and waiting. Mama chopped the unsuspecting chickens' heads off on the old chopping block out by the woodpile. The headless chickens flopped around, all over the place, and almost made you think they would run away. We held each chicken by the feet and dipped them up and down in a bucket of scalding hot water to loosen the feathers. Plucking those feathers proved to be a nasty smelly job, but each of us knew we had to help. The thought of Mama's fried chicken, chicken and dumplings, and chicken salad sandwiches helped us forge ahead with our gruesome job.

When the chickens passed Mama's inspection she held each one over the fire to singe the pin-feathers, then removed the feet and rinsed each chicken in clean water. After several washings the chickens were ready to be cut and put into a tub of ice cold water, waiting to be cooked, fried, or canned for future use.

Cutting the chicken open and removing the internal parts took skill to prevent contaminating the meat. Mama was the chicken cutter. She knew just where to cut to remove the liver, the gizzard, and other parts. She was also a great teacher. She showed us how chickens digested their food different from other animals and people. Sometimes the hens would have a surprise inside of them—an egg that was fully developed. We learned about science and the facts of life without even realizing it. Mama cut up each chicken the same way every time, as everyone in the family had their favorite piece. We looked forward to our turn at making a wish on the wishbone.

Hogs provided the main source of meat for us. If we did butcher a steer or cow before we had a freezer, Mama had to can the meat in jars to keep it from spoiling. We butchered hogs every year, and that meat was cured, smoked, or canned until the 1960's when Daddy bought Mama a big deep freezer.

Hog butchering day was much more involved than chicken butchering. It rated right up there with the other holidays like Easter and Christmas. It always took place in late fall or early winter to be sure the cold temperatures would keep the meat from spoiling. A well-stocked smokehouse was a must for a large family.

The smokehouse was an enchanting place filled with the sweet smell of the sugar-cure. The rows and rows of dangling sausages, the large bulky hams, shoulders, and bacons wrapped in white cloth, and the huge crocks of lard, covered with oilcloth, provided security for the long cold months ahead. We couldn't wait for that first meal of thickly sliced sugar-cured ham, mounds of creamy mashed potatoes, light-as-a-feather biscuits spread with churned butter and blackberry jelly, and Mama's milk gravy. Life was good.

Aside from the meat, milk, and eggs, the bulk of the rest of our diet came from Mama's garden and the bounty of nature. I called it Mama's garden because she decided what to plant and where to plant everything. Daddy took care of the plowing and fertilizing which required the use of our horses and a two-bottom plow, until we moved up in the world and got a tractor.

A big garden requires a lot of work. My three sisters and I learned at a very early age to drop potato pieces just the right distance apart in the long trenches that Mama made, then ridge the dirt over them, at planting time. Hoeing, weeding, and harvesting food from the garden involved all of us, and we knew it was no use to complain, as we certainly enjoyed eating. And we clearly remembered Daddy reading the passage in the Bible that says, "He that does not work, neither shall he eat."

Mama let each of us girls pick out our favorite flower seeds, which we planted all around the edges of the huge garden. "Pretty flowers are God's way of rewarding us for all our hard work." reminded Mama. "It also gives you something beautiful to look at while you work." she added. A great number of vegetables filled Mama's garden, but we were especially attentive to our favorites— watermelon, cantaloupe, popcorn and peanuts.

Nature provided many foods that required no hoeing, tilling, and fertilizing on our part. Black-berries, dewberries, elderberries, wild grapes, wild plums, persimmons, walnuts, and hickory nuts were just a few of the abundance of God-given foods free for the taking. We made treks to the woods and fencerows, each carrying our own bucket or basket as we looked for nature's treasures. These outings not only brought us many good things to eat but also brought us closer together as a family.

Being a part of the growth and production of the family farm has been a blessing in my life.

Sharing the farm duties under the gentle guidance of my parents provided me with a roadmap for becoming a parent and made me a stronger and more self-confident person. The satisfaction of jobs well done inspired me to become a self-sufficient, dependable caretaker of God's creation.

The Gift
by C.A. Simonson

I was about to exit the Special Care unit of the Veterans Home where the residents with Alzheimer's and other types of dementia lived. It was a locked unit; staff coming and leaving had to know the secret code of the number lock pad to get in or out. I had to be cautious and very quick, for sly patients would follow me to the door to watch my fingers, hoping to decipher the code and hope for escape. They were sure they had to go home.

As part of the social worker's team, I finished playing piano for the weekly sing-along time with the residents and prepared to go back to my office. As I walked toward the locked doors, a frail, bent-over man with frizzy white hair and wild-looking eyes followed close behind. His mumbled words and crazy gibberish made him seem deranged and scary.

Stay away from him, I was warned. *He will try to grab you in places he shouldn't.* I turned to see him coming toward me rather quickly for an octogenarian with arms outstretched and a cockeyed grin on his face. I quickened my steps, but I was too slow. He caught up with me.

The old man gently grabbed my arm, and turned me so I would face him. He put both hands tenderly on my face, and looked into my eyes.

What now? I wondered, half-fearful. *I had heard stories about this guy. Should I call for a nurse?* Instead, I quieted myself and stood my ground. He didn't look harmful. I smiled at the man and waited. He cleared his throat.

"I remembered the words today," he whispered, his words clear and slow. Then a tear slipped from his eye. With that, he smiled at me, turned around and walked back to his room.

I stood trembling at what just happened. Though he couldn't remember his own name most of the time and didn't remember where he lived, the old man was so pleased he could remember the words of the hymns. His words, the first intelligible ones I had ever heard him speak, were a special gift to me that day—a gift I would treasure forever.

Thumb and Forefinger
by James Coffman

I was 15 and not a criminal. I promise, 8 years on the west side of Indianapolis and not a single scratch or bruise marred my reputation.

Things happen, like the young policeman one block from us who obliterated our baseball field by digging a huge square hole between home plate and second base and then moved his 2-story house over the basement. I learned, then, that actions have consequences and one thing follows another no matter how pure your intentions.

Without our having guessed it, a few friends and I unwittingly became the victims of a big city sting, vintage 1955. On two sides of the policeman's new home sere seated—on their front porches—about twelve innocent neighbors, who in the interest of law and order, had promised the policeman that whenever the unruly youths of the 3300 hundred block of Wilcox St. came onto the property again, Mr. Longarm would get a call.

The irony was that even if we had explored before this day—from underneath and inside—we had not transgressed today. Nevertheless, the "concerned citizens" had pulled the trigger and a chain of events was set into motion.

We've all heard police sirens from the safety of our homes or front porches, but this one was personal. For the first and only time in my life, I heard a police siren which was mine.

I was able to look past all this drama; I was old enough to know that it was only to scare me. So, none of this bothered me…. too much. What did bother me? Would you believe my mother's thumb and forefinger clamped tightly onto my left ear as she pulled me—literally—down Wilcox St. Never in my 15 years had she resorted to this medieval treatment. It was on this day—with a dozen neighbors sitting on their front porches—my mother acted as the aggrieved mom with commentary, "Jim, we never raised you like this. I am appalled!"

Her voice was louder than necessary, meant for the neighbors seated on their curved metal red and green lawn chairs—staring nonchalantly upward as if bored to tears.

Would A Thong Have Gone So Wrong?
by Lynn Strand McIntosh

Recently several in our family stayed at an upscale hotel for a family wedding. The breakfast included was not your typical scrambled eggs and Styrofoam setting. Guests were actually seated at tables with silverware and the bountiful buffet was served at one end behind a screen attendant with fresh offerings.

Each morning a text alerted us Grandparents that our grandsons were up and the mad dash to corral them for breakfast had begun. We dressed quickly, grabbed our keys and joined the parade. It took at least four adults to wrangle a buffet breakfast for three boys. Mom and Dad were scrambling for eggs while my husband and I balanced plates, got juices and made relays to the buffet. Tables were always full at this popular hotel and guests were waiting to be seated. The second day, after our buffet buffeting, my husband and I stayed a few more minutes to quietly finish our coffee. We discussed the pleasant accommodations and resplendent breakfast. I mentioned I was personally glad I had upped my wardrobe for our stay as we signed our ticket and left an adequate tip for our family's messy gluttony.

Walking around the register, I felt something at the back of my knee. We were not yet to the hallway and I bent down to see what had brushed against me. My underwear! Neon pink balled up granny pants were sticking out of my capris! I quickly grabbed the worrisome wad and stuffed it in the back of my pants. Recovering from this deft move I looked over my shoulder to see at least one gentleman honed in on the action. I turned to my husband and told him my underwear was falling out of my pants. He passively asked what I meant. As we rounded the corner by ourselves I pulled the wad from my back and showed him. As a man's thought process does not include used underwear hanging about the knees in public, he was speechless. How many times had I walked to the buffet or attended the kids at the table bending over to butter toast or pour syrup? Did he recall any pointing, giggling or throwing up?

I had taken the pants off to take a shower the night before and then grabbed them that morning for breakfast. Maybe I should consider thongs, I never thought I would like the gluteal channel breaker, but at least I would know where they were and a thong would have been slight enough to not be unsightly! I wondered when that pink pile peeked out of my jeans; when it might happen again; when will they make me stay home; or when will they put me under lock and key?

Photograph by Ida Fogle

FICTION 2016

Cellar Dweller
by Frank Montagnino

First Place

Renaldo Cruz found the key while rummaging through drawers in the kitchen looking for a beer opener. It seemed out of place because it was the only key in a drawer full of kitchen odds and ends, so he asked the landlady, Mrs. Swenson, what the key opened. She had gotten very defensive about it, grabbing the key away from him and bustling down the hall to her bedroom all the while mumbling something about the basement. He had shrugged the whole thing off, putting it down to Mrs. Swenson's age or senility or something.

Renaldo. had forgotten about the key until one day when he'd gone into the kitchen to get a cup of Mrs. Swenson's rancid black coffee. He was pouring the coffee when he heard a scratching noise coming from behind the basement door. It sounded like a cat or some other kind of animal. He had put his ear to the door, listening hard, but the scratching had stopped. Renaldo turned the doorknob at which point he heard a scurrying noise as if the cat or whatever it was had been frightened back down the stairs into the basement. He'd stood there a few minutes, but heard nothing more. As he turned from the door he'd been startled to see Mrs. Swenson standing there. "Just getting some coffee, Mrs. Swenson," he'd mumbled nervously. She hadn't said a word, just stared at him as he had slunk past her and gone back up to his room.

Renaldo couldn't stop thinking about the basement. Every time he walked through the kitchen (if Mrs. Swenson wasn't there) he tried the knob on the basement door. He'd even begun dreaming about what Mrs. Swenson might be hiding down there. What could it be? It couldn't be a pet. People don't go to the expense and trouble of having a pet only to keep it locked away where they could never see it or play with it. It couldn't be a guard dog. A guard dog locked away in the basement couldn't be much help. But if not a pet, what could it be? Finally, Renaldo's obsession had grown so much he decided that next time he had a chance he'd have to see for himself.

One night at supper, Mrs. Swenson announced she was leaving in the morning to visit her daughter and that she'd be gone for the whole day. Next morning, immediately after he heard her slam the front door, Renaldo crept down the stairs and straight into Mrs. Swenson's bedroom. He found the key in a wooden jewelry case atop the bureau and in seconds he had inserted it into the lock on the basement door. Quickly, before he lost his nerve, he turned the key, twisted the knob, jerked the door open and jumped back three paces. Nothing there. He was breathing quickly, almost panting and he wiped perspiration from his forehead as he looked at the darkness inside the door frame.

To switch on the basement light, he had to reach inside the door frame and he needed a few minutes to work himself up to that. As he was standing there, Renaldo looked for scratches on the inside of the door. He found them, but not near the base of the door where a cat or dog would have made them. These scratches were almost at eye height. "Must be a big dog," he muttered to himself, "like a Great Dane or an Irish Wolfhound." He shuddered at the thought of encountering a big, hungry dog that had been locked up in a basement for God knows how long. A thought came to him and he went to the refrigerator and took a couple of slices out of a package of bologna. "Don't eat me dog," he muttered. "I come bearing gifts."

Armed with the bologna, Renaldo went back to the door, reached in and threw the light switch. A lone, naked bulb hanging halfway down the staircase dimly illuminated the stairs. Slowly, cautiously, Renaldo forced himself down the stairs to the basement floor. Two more bare light bulbs concentrated light in the middle of the basement. From the foot of the steps he could see the usual basement clutter, furnace, water heater, several sets of shelves loaded with miscellany. The shelves stuck out at right angles from the basement walls leaving more darkened hiding places.

"Anyone down here," he called, his voice cracking with nervousness. There was no reply, but he heard a slight scuttling somewhere in the dark. He froze, listening, imagining, wondering when the monster would come crashing out of the dark. Finally, after minutes that seemed like hours, his aching legs forced him to move. Eyes wide, the bologna crushed in his grip, he inched forward, coming abreast of the first set of shelves. There in the shadows he saw the form wedged in the angle between the shelves and the wall. It was as tall as he was although crouched in a submissive posture. The thing seemed to be covered in hair or perhaps it was dirty rags. As his eyes became more accustomed to the dim light he saw that the form seemed to have its back toward him and was hiding its face. It was almost as though this hairy thing was as afraid of Renaldo as Renaldo was afraid of it. The thought gave him a dash of courage.

"Hello," he croaked. "My name is Renaldo. What's your name?" At the sound of Renaldo's voice, the creature shuddered, tried to press itself even further into the wall. It issued a low, mournful moan.

The moan and the creature's non-aggressive manner emboldened Renaldo. He bent over, hands on his knees, like he was talking to a child. "I'm not going to hurt you," he cooed. "I live upstairs. Mrs. Swenson lives upstairs too. Do you know Mrs. Swenson.?"

The creature moaned again, louder this time.

Mrs. Swenson owns this house," Renaldo went on, feeling as though he had to keep talking. The creature turned to face him. As it moved into the light Renaldo could see two eyes peering from behind a huge bush of hair. It was human. Strange, hairy, but definitely human.

Feeling rather silly, he pointed to himself and said, "Me Renaldo." Then pointing toward the man-creature he said, "You?" The thing said nothing, but slowly reached out an emaciated arm. Only then did Renaldo realize he had been gesturing with the hand holding the bologna.

"Are you hungry?" he asked, extending the bologna even farther. Tentatively, the creature reached out and Renaldo could see its long, filthy, claw-like fingernails. He also saw the iron manacle and its trailing chain attached to the creature's wrist. The thing took the bologna and jammed it into its mouth, devouring it in seconds.

"Well, you were hungry," Renaldo remarked. "I'll get some more." He turned and trotted up the steps to the kitchen, returning a moment later with the rest of the lunch meat and a box of crackers. He put the bologna and a few crackers on the floor, positioned so the creature would have to come out into the light to get them. Slowly the creature crawled out from behind the shelves, dragging his chain behind him and hunched over the food. In the light, Renaldo could see that the creature was a youngish man dressed in filthy, tattered clothes that were at least two sizes too small. His hair reached to his waist and was the same dirty color as the rags he wore. Renaldo wondered how long would it take for hair to grow that long? Must have been years.

"How long have you been down here?" Renaldo asked. "Is Mrs. Swenson keeping you down here?"

The man started rocking back and forth, obviously agitated. He held out his shackled arm and with his other hand shook the chain, holding it out for Renaldo to see.

"Is Mrs. Swenson your mother?"

With that the man loosed a horrible scream and leapt to his feet as Renaldo cowered back. He grabbed his chain with both hands and bashed it time and again onto the concrete and into the shelves until, exhausted, he fell to the floor moaning and rocking.

Uncertain as to what to do next, Renaldo shook a few more crackers onto the floor. As the creature reached out for the food the rags that passed for clothing parted revealing a collection of welts and healed scars on its bony arm. Renaldo pointed to the creature's arm.

"Did Mrs. Swenson do that to you," he asked, not really expecting a reply. The man-thing began rocking and moaning again. Then the creature pivoted on its haunches turning his back to Renaldo. Slowly it reached its claw-like hands behind its neck and started inching the ragged shirt upward. Renaldo stared at the jagged lettering formed by unattended scars. There, in a diagonal line carved into the creature's back from his left shoulder to his right hip was the word *U-N-W-A-N-T-E-D*.

"That monstrous bitch," Renaldo cursed as the enormity of what he was seeing came into focus. Mrs. Swenson had not only imprisoned this poor creature in her cellar for years and years, she had inflicted this and God knows what other kinds of torture on the unfortunate soul. That the wretch before him was Mrs. Swenson's own son made the whole scenario even more nightmarish.

The man-thing swung back around to face Renaldo. He pointed

upward toward the ceiling and then began pounding one fist into the other hand. It growled as it pounded, harder and harder with each blow punctuated by a gesture pointing to the ceiling. Eventually the man tired and sat breathing heavily on the cold concrete floor. Renaldo got to his feet and began pacing. What to do? Obviously this horrible situation had to end, but how? He could call the police of course, but his own record made him reluctant to do so. No, he reasoned, whatever was to be done it was best if Renaldo Cruz was never implicated.

Although it had never mattered before he was suddenly grateful that Mrs. Swenson had demanded rent payment in cash. There was no rental contract that would link him to this house. If he gathered his few belongings and left, there would be no sign he had ever lived here. As he paced he noticed the coil of chain the creature had pulled away from its anchor in the wall. The scratches on the kitchen door proved there was enough chain to reach that far, but no farther. He shuddered at the vision of this enraged man-thing should it ever get his claws on the cause of his torment. Then he smiled.

Renaldo rummaged around the junk-filled basement and found a box of tools. In a few moments he had chiseled the chain anchor loose from the concrete wall. Although it didn't realize it, the man-thing was free.

Renaldo emptied the remainder of the box of crackers on the cellar floor and while the creature was devouring them he wiped down the hammer and chisel. He then went back up the steps, turned off the light and closed and locked the door. In his room he crammed his things into his duffle. He made the bed then carefully wiped the lamp, the drawer handles, the door knob and anything he might have touched. He did the same in the bathroom, then in the kitchen. When he was finished he checked his watch. Five o'clock. Mrs. Swenson would be back very soon. He smiled at the thought of what awaited her.

The last thing Renaldo Cruz did before he left Mrs. Swenson's boarding house was to carefully put the key in the middle of the kitchen table where he knew she'd see it.

Spider Bite
by Susannah Albert-Chandhok

Two microscopic holes appeared in the wrinkled groove above her wrist. An influx of putrid yellow toxin compressed itself through the infinitesimal tunnel, first condensed as droplets with solid, infinite surfaces. Then, as the toxin burst in the industrial red river below her skin, the poison deliquesced into a fungal, grotesque swill.

The pain of the invisible drilling compelled her gaze, but she was too late in brushing the spider away. Her blood instantaneously succumbed to the noxious tsunami tearing through her arm. She watched as the wrinkles behind her wrists, these indentations that formed over a lifetime of handshakes and brushing away tears, of handholding and of one well-deserved punch, distended. The cells in her arm could do nothing more than mitigate the pain of her swelling arm. The numbness was brief. A short inhale.

On her exhale, the toxin punched through her shoulder. She felt an army of adrenaline meet the enemy, but the battle was short. Death by poison was blitzkrieg. The invader engulfed her heart, and the blood from her final heartbeat congealed. Her knees, in their last act, bent, as if surrendering might appease the act of dying.

Her heart stopped, but she wasn't dead. Her life was a caesura. Her eyes, frozen open without blood flowing to shut them, concentrated on a pinpoint of darkness on the muddy ground.

It was her murderer. This spider, she realized, would be the last life form she ever encountered. In that way, despite being her executioner, the spider was exceptional. She thought of the people who had been the most important in her life—her parents, her siblings, her husband—and even the animal most important to her, her cat for the last twelve years. These other living creatures had impacted her, yet even her favorite ones had hurt her. The time her mother had said she was disappointed in her. When her husband, a few months before he would propose, told her that he was leaving her. Even her cat adored flexing his claws into his owner's skin, leaving marks bigger than the holes that were currently killing her.

She decided to extend her curiosity to the spider, a creature whose influence in her life was most consequential. Her immediate reaction was to feel only abhorrence. If her wrists weren't useless slabs of dough, she would want to smash the spider. She would have reveled as its innards exploded. In movies, she thought, your death was noble as long as you killed the person who killed you.

At once, her heart, no longer a working muscle, softened. Was the spider really her enemy?

Minutes before, she had been walking down a wilderness trail, barely visible under blanket of dead leaves. She stopped to let a jogger pass her on the left, and then indulged her idleness after the jogger's steps muted. She found that that the *crunch-crunch* of feet had been replaced by the *dee-dee-dee* of birds and *zut-zut* of squirrels. She didn't grimace when the cold air bit her ears for she was content breathing in the silence that wasn't silent at all.

During her consumption of the present moment, she realized her shoelace was untied. She hopped with her left foot and extended her right foot out toward a nearby tree. But she misjudged and lost her balance. Her instability wasn't severe. She had instinctually reached out her arms for safety, but if she hadn't, she wouldn't have fallen. Her hand fell against the tree, and she didn't immediately pull away.

What had the spider seen as her hand pushed into the bark? A weapon? A fleshy tank preparing for combat? She suddenly respected the spider. It was a martyr. The spider must have known that survival was impossible when encountering an armament ten times its size with a punch of two hundred pounds of force. She couldn't have communicated her intentions to the spider, and the spider had to assume the worst.

Who had the spider been protecting? Its children? Its web? The tree? Maybe the spider lay down its life to defend all the living creatures that called that tree home. Perhaps the spider wasn't protecting anything at all, but its survival instincts, which had kept its ancestors alive throughout global catastrophes and the arrival of OFF!, had kicked in at that exact moment. For the spider to make it to this moment in time, the moment of the bite, the spider must have had the most courageous forefathers who exhibited the most intelligent and fittest of behaviors.

What if the tree had always been this spider's home? She had recently moved to this city, following her husband's new job, and had learned about this wilderness trail through asking her cell phone. The trail itself was 2.4 miles long and popular because its path led to wonderful views of a cave system that speleologists still study today. The land that the trail branched through had originally been owned by ranchers, going back to the time of the early Western explorers, who had taken the land from Native Americans, who maybe had taken the land from a herd of buffalo or deer…could it go back as far as the mammoths? Had a mother mammoth engaged in a similar showdown with spider thousands of years ago? Who was the invader—the spider or the mammoth?

Her eyesight remained on the spider, but her brain struggled to convert light waves into meaningful images.

Yes, she could respect this tiny creature, admire its tenacity, and comprehend its instinct to kill her. In her final moments, she challenged herself with a question: could she love this spider?

The spider was alive and, for these final moments, so was she. Was there a spirit, something beyond molecules and even quarks, connecting all life forms? She was happy about her life, maybe not about every part, but she was thankful to have been alive. Could she appreciate all life forms because she was grateful for her own existence?

And when death overtook her existence and left her body to decompose over time, wouldn't the minerals and molecules that had given her life be consumed by an earthworm or the roots of a sheaf of grass to fuel continued livelihood on Earth? Could she assume that she and the spider shared the minerals and molecules from the death of a singular earlier being? In fact, the spider and she must share elements from a star that had supernovaed billions of years ago or else neither would exist at all. Therefore, the two were celestial siblings. Could she find peace, in her final moment, of loving the spider, her kin?

"No, I promise you that you would not be at peace with a spider if it bit you," her husband said as they walked down the trail, hand in hand. "You made me squash that moth the other day, and it wasn't even doing anything except decorating our bathroom wall!"

"Yes," she said. "But I needed to take a shower, and I was worried about it attacking me when I was vulnerable like that."

"A moth would do a lot less harm," he said.

"Still," she responded, "I'd prefer to die from a spider bite than be crushed by a boulder."

Secrets of a Shapeshifter
by Laura Seabaugh

The new territory wasn't so bad. The scent of smoke lingered in Kantile's mind, but here the pines were fresh and green, banishing the memory with their own sweet fragrance. The cool air soothed the sting from her eyes and throat. And her feet fell on wildflowers instead of embers. Definitely an improvement.

Tracks in the earth showed evidence of rainfall and, even better: *life*. New growth on the trees held promise that this terrain was done with its quakes and eruptions and firestorms, at least for now. Such were the quandaries of a new world, but that wasn't something Kantile could hold against it. She was new once, too.

It would have been better to explore by air, especially since nothing was better than flying. Kantile reveled in the view, not to mention the thrill, but her only flying forms were mere songbirds at best and she knew any one of the resident hawks would make a quick meal of her. She didn't really want to get eaten.

As a raccoon, she climbed over every knoll and root, around every rock, stump and fallen log, as fast as her little feet could carry her. Plenty of creatures ate raccoons, sure, but she could change her mimicry to another ground form—maybe badger or lynx, or whichever proved most appropriate for an encounter—without the inherent complication of falling.

That was the trouble with being a shapeshifter. She had to get close to something to memorize its shape, and the best forms were particularly dangerous. Like griffons. All she needed was one feather. Even a small, downy one would do, but she didn't know any forms that could get close to the beasts, territorial as they were with their nests and their mountains. Someday she would make that endeavor.

For the time being, a raccoon form would suffice, being big enough to cover ground, yet small enough to go unnoticed. The only problem now was that something smelled delightfully like fish and she couldn't think of anything but food. As long as the smell kept luring her east, it would increase her distance from the fire-breathing bullfrogs of the old territory, and that was all that really mattered.

She nosed through the underbrush and scaled a fallen log out of the shrubbery for a better view. The land spread out from the edge of the forest in a range of rolling hills. A single column of smoke rose out of a copse not far away. It looked suspicious, being a product of fire, but Kantile was always guilty of being more curious than cautious.

The angle of sunlight through the trees heralded the coming dusk, the time a real raccoon would become active. Kantile ventured downhill, trying to keep an ear out for predators over the rumbling of her own stomach. The breeze still carried the promise of fish through the pines, but there was an unfamiliarity about it that made the shapeshifter uneasy. It reminded her of the burning earth, the singed trees and stink of cataclysm she wanted to keep behind her.

She slowed her pace as the odor became sharper, close and pungent through the young trees. The hill bottomed out, opening on a clearing where an odd collection of sticks and rocks lay about the trampled ground. It got weirder as she sidled closer to investigate a cave made of some kind of animal hide stripped from its body. Every hair on her back stood up as she pondered how that could be.

The source of the smoke was contained within a pit dug out of the ground in a most conspicuous fashion. Sticks and bones carved into tools littered the ground around it. The fish she found skewered over a pile of smoking twigs, the strangest thing she'd ever encountered since the evolution of frogs. Most things in the world made sense to Kantile. Frogs and smoking fish did not.

In spite of herself, she had to try this smoky fish and see if it tasted as good as it smelled. She crept toward the pit. Sniffed the air. Then, stretching up on her hind feet, she tested one of the smaller filets with her teeth. The heat of it startled her into dropping the fish in the dirt. She was about to try again when she heard a sound from the trees.

Not to be chased from her prize, she snapped up the fish in her mouth and scampered off into the underbrush just as someone with two legs stepped into the clearing. His skin was the color of the earth, his eyes dark with mischief. He skipped toward the fire pit and made vocalizations curiously strung together.

Humans! But these were different from the humans Kantile remembered. This one stood taller, with more intelligence and less hair. Others followed. Some of them carried pockets of greens or berries. Some brought broken tree branches and added them to the fire. Many returned only with their empty woven things and disappointment on their faces.

One of the females trudged separately behind the others. She had a gangly, adolescent gait exaggerated by her scrawny limbs. Her hair was straggly in contrast to the thick locks of her kin. Stranger still was the muddy thing she wore over her eyes.

Someone stopped her as she neared the fire. He was a large human in rags of animal skins and his hand looked enormous around her wrist. His heavy brow shaded his eyes in a deepening frown as he pointed at the smoking fish. Even as he spoke to her in their simple language, she kept her face down. When he pushed her backward, she folded to the earth on the edge of their camp and sat.

The rest of the tribe ignored her and passed around the fish, from the oldest and strongest among them to the youngest and weakest. They left none for her.

Kantile looked down at the fish she'd taken, now cool on the ground at her feet. She usually avoided humans. The grunting, scratching dimwits that populated areas of the old territory seemed harmless until they started thinking they were superior to other animals. Human behavior baffled her, and after a few unsettling encounters, she deemed it best to avoid them altogether.

Now she felt something she wasn't used to feeling and had no experience in handling. She didn't see anything wrong with eating a piece of fish left to chance and elements. In the wild, all food was fair game. Now, for some reason, it didn't seem right for her to eat it.

It wasn't her fault the tribe shunned one of its own, but it didn't make sense, even for humans. The girl wasn't lame or deformed. If she could walk, she could find water and hunt, if not for that thing around her head. It didn't slow her down when the matriarch cuffed her ear and sent her scrambling off into the woods.

Kantile crept around the camp toward the other side where the girl disappeared, keeping an eye on the humans from the safety of the grass. They were so possessive of a piece of fish that she'd hate to find out what they'd do if they discovered her. She scrambled through the weeds and caught up with the girl in a little tangle of shrubs just outside the glow from the fire.

The girl hunched in the grasses near a tree, looking more like a stunned rabbit than a sentient being. With her eyes covered, she didn't react when Kantile padded out of hiding and sat in front of her.

One of the benefits of being a raccoon was that raccoons had dexterous little paws, so she was able to peel the muddy wrap of hide from around the girl's head. The human blinked and rubbed dirt off her brow. She studied Kantile through a frown.

That was when Kantile noticed the girl's eyes were two entirely different colors. The shapeshifter stared back, wondering if it was a trick of the light. The girl's left eye was definitely blue, a deepwater blue, but her right eye glinted green in the faint glow from the fire. Kantile was so intrigued that she stood up on her hind legs for a better look.

Now the girl decided to be startled, falling on her rump and scooting backward. Kantile turned and shambled away to get the fish she'd left on the ground. The girl would want her fish. Kantile could give it back. Or maybe they could share it. No, no, the human was hungrier. Kantile retrieved the fish and shuffled closer to the girl with it hanging lopsided from her mouth.

It might have had a little drool on it, but the girl was unfazed as she bit into the silvery flesh. Kantile licked her chops, testing the remnant oils on her tongue. She couldn't decide if she liked the flavor of fire. The girl stopped mid-bite and broke off a piece, holding it out on her fingers.

They shared the fish and with it, a wordless understanding. The girl ate without reserve and for a while the only sounds were cricket songs accompanied by tree frogs. Kantile accepted her spare bites, savoring each little taste of humanity.

Her transformation was seamless. She didn't always get to share in the tokens that defined a creature, gave it form. Birds shed feathers and squirrels misplaced acorns, but most creatures didn't *possess* things, not even food. Kantile could have eaten the stolen fish, but it wouldn't have been the same. And while it was easier to consume her tokens than to carry them with her, they were never shared or given freely. Taking the girl's form was effortless. Kantile hardly felt it happening. It was a part of her now.

The girl gasped, mismatched eyes flaring wide.

Alarmed and a little embarrassed, Kantile raised a human finger to her lips and sat back on her heels. "Don't be afraid," she whispered. The words rolled off her tongue, her human tongue. She knew language, knew the languages of birds and insects and beasts, but not this one. This one was unfamiliar, but it came with the form, like the dirt and the scars and the clothes. Clothes. She was wearing clothes! She couldn't help giggling.

The girl was curious, gesturing and reaching out experimentally. Kantile imitated her movements, waving when she waved, sticking out her tongue when she stuck out her tongue. Their little game stretched into the night until a shout tore through the crickets' revelry and silence settled over the trees. The girl reached for her blindfold.

Kantile swiped it from her and threw it into the weeds. She stood, ready to move, but the patriarch from the camp spotted her. As he started tromping toward Kantile, the other girl also rose. Something about the sight of them made him stop short. His eyes got big. Kantile, in human form, should have understood the language, but most of the noises he made were incomprehensible. When he turned back toward his camp, a few of the others raised their voices in confusion.

The girl stared after him, but Kantile couldn't let her go back to those people. She liked this human. She didn't like to see her fall victim to the superstitious tendencies of her kind. The two of them could make their own way together. It would be an adventure.

She took her new friend by the hand. The girl glanced from her to the camp and back at her, but there was a glint of something hopeful in her mismatched eyes. The rocks whipping through the foliage in their general direction probably meant they should start their adventure in a hurry. Running on two feet was awkward for Kantile at first, but she would adapt. She always did.

A Telling Moment in a Changing Life
by Kit Salter

Jake sat on the bar stool he favored at the kitchen counter. He was alone. The late news was almost over. He could hear from his daughter's bedroom down the hall the droning grim-faced newscasters finishing their nightly litany of shootings and robbery reports with mug shots. It was those faces that made viewers feel damn glad they were watching from home and not facing these low-lifes on the street or in parking lots. Sports was done and only the weather recap remained.

In the kitchen, Jake looked down at his gnarly hands circling the coffee cup. That word—gnarly—was exactly right for the folds of skin, liver spots and scars that went from his fingertips to his medic bracelet. A Goodwill Carhartt shirt covered up his early tattoos that marched up his forearms to biceps. Biceps? He used to be proud of that word. Now he called them his "goodbye-ceps" that had replaced the youthful real biceps he used to show off with his tee shirt and pack of cigarettes rolled up in the sleeve. This sorry reality was all part of the folly of the so-called Golden Years. The whole goddam package was a sham.

He sat at this kitchen counter when he came up from his basement quarters to 'interact' with his daughter and her dweeb husband. Jake toyed with the idea of getting a touch of Bourbon to sweeten the taste of the cold coffee from the dinner pot, but he thought better of it—'Don't give 'em anything to use in their battle against my life as it ought to be,' he told himself. He saw the clock circling toward 10:30. He'd get their attention before they segued into one of the Late Night Jimmy shows. Jake tried to suppress the fact that he was brimming with irritation as he called out his question.

"Becky…can we talk a few minutes?"

Down the hall, the television went silent.

"Ya don't need to kill the tube. I just got one question. You'll still make the monologue."

He heard her steps coming down the hall from their bedroom, probably with Howard close behind her.

From the hallway she asked, "What is it, Dad? Howard and I thought you'd gone to bed already."

"No, I haven't gone to bed. It's barely 10:30. I want to go to Leroy's."

There was a pause in her movement toward the kitchen. Jake had an image of her husband bumping into her as she paused abruptly in response to his question.

"Is Leroy's still open this late, Dad?"

"Well, yeah…it's a bar, a road house. It doesn't keep library hours."

"Is someone coming to pick you up?" Becky had come to the kitchen doorway as she asked this question.

"No. No one is coming to pick me up. I want to pick me up and drive me the four miles to Leroy's. Then I want to have a single beer. Then I want to drive me back to my basement doorway. Park my truck. And come in and go to bed in the flea market bunk you and Howard put in the basement."

Becky was playing with her hair. She was wearing some sort of robe that looked as though it would be better placed in a 1950s diorama labeled "Evenings of Elegance in the Fifty's." It could be in any storefront window on any declining small town Main Street. There were hundreds—maybe thousands—of them.

"This is a bad time to raise this issue, Dad. You know Howard and I get to bed after the news because we both have jobs. Jobs, Dad. We both work. We both leave the house, go to work, work all day, come home and keep the house going. Our day doesn't have the grand flexibility you gained by quitting the part time job you had at Home Depot after retiring from the Post Office."

"You an' Howard don't need to get involved in any of this, Becky. All you have to do is give me my truck keys, kiss me on the cheek and tell me to Drive Carefully and go back up the hall to your bedroom. Then you can rest for p-r-e-p-a-r-i-n-g to go to work." Jake stood up from his counter stool and extended his arm.

Becky was now fully in the kitchen with Howard standing next to her. He was perhaps two inches taller than Jake's daughter, but he did not fill space with the same gravity she did. She pulled her robe more tightly around her body as she spoke.

"Dad…we've had this conversation too many times. It just cannot become a regular nighttime or morning time or all-the-time discussion. Howard and I have been watching your driving ever since you backed into that ditch over at Neill's farm. It was no big thing, but it was careless…in fact it was stupid. And driving stupid's something that you hollered at me not to do all the years I drove as a teenager. Now you're 79 and doing exactly that." She paused and then went on. "A month ago you drove your truck over one of those concrete parking lot pylons and we had to get Triple A to pull you off it…"

"No…you two called the damn tow service before you gave me a chance to work my way off that half-assed barrier. The grocery store ought to be taken to court for having placed those damn things every which way around the parking lot. They're probably in cahoots with AAA and split the fees people ring up as they're planning on leaving the lot but instead get hung up on those useless things." It was clear that this was not a new conversation.

"Right. You've said that many times…but I still call it stupid driving not to know where you're going when you launch off for home or Leroy's or the Senior Center." Before Jake could respond, Howard spoke.

"Jake, these distractions are confusing the way you drive and that makes me and Becky worried for your safety—and all this endless 'Can I have my keys?' talk makes me crazy." He seemed to be standing just a little taller as he spoke for the first time.

"Bullshit, I say to that. I've driven more than a million miles with only a few accidents—and only one was serious—and that wasn't my fault. What I want now is the right to drive my truck to Leroy's for a beer and then drive home—an 8 mile round trip—on a quiet night. No snow. No rain. No animals in the truck. No agenda except me trying like hell to keep some say in my own shrinking life. You two have me assigned to the basement and it feels like a Preparation Zone for a Twilight Days Assisted Living sequence. And once I'm dumped in there I sure as hell won't have any independence. What I want now is to be able to ease myself into the full rapture of my friggin' golden years by driving alone on these little trips that neither of you would ever want to make."

Jake quickly put his hand up silencing a response from Becky.

"Or, how about this, Becky—you have Howard drive me to Leroy's. He could come in and play with his cell phone while I talk with a buddy who still talks instead of texts?"

Howard began to reply but Becky broke in. "No, Dad…we're not running a nighttime taxi service. WE WORK. If you want a beer at 10:30 why don't you call a so-called 'buddy' and have him pick you up and bring you home?"

Jake glowered at his childless daughter. "Oh, yeah…like a Play Date when the kid is 5 or 6. Do you have any idea what it feels like for me to call a friend and ask him to pick me up so we can go get a beer at night? I've grown up with most of these guys at Leroy's and having to do a Call Around to find wheels to the bar is so blessed humiliating I can't bring myself to do it. Hell, I'm in better shape than most of them and yet I'm the one who can't come out to play."

There was an awkward silence. Then Howard stepped forward a foot in from the kitchen doorway and spoke. "Becky, I'm sick as hell of this continual bitching from your Dad about how we have made him a Kept Man. Let's give him his truck keys and take back our own independence." For a few seconds, this declaration stunned both Jake and Becky. Howard continued. "Jake—You take your damn keys. Schedule your own stuff. Just know that when you've rolled into a ditch and call, or killed a cow on Sycamore Road, you have to figure things out yourself. Having you live with us was Becky's idea, just like having you turn over your keys because you're losing your driving edge BUT you don't see that. So, from now on, I'm NOT going to see that either."

By the time Howard had finished his surprising monologue he seemed fully as tall as Becky. She had not moved since her generally quiet husband had called for the policy change. Jake stared at the man in his pajamas. Becky turned to her husband.

"Howard…you know there's no half-way in this sort of thing. Either we take responsibility for Dad's driving, or we don't. If we give him back his truck keys, then we're the ones who will be called when he runs a light and crashes into an old lady making a slow turn out of the church parking lot or something. Are you ready for that?"

"Hell, Becky," Jake responded, "I'm not going to cream some old lady's car. I still see just fine. It's only that sometimes I get caught up in all of the stuff coming down the pike my way as I crowd 80. Growing old is a load of crap."

"No, Dad, that's not going to do it. You own up to the need to be a thinking driver or you get on the phone and line up Beer Nights with your buddies who have not done stupid things with their trucks. Let them be your wheels. Howard and I are not sanctioning Driving With Excuses. If you get your keys, it'll be Driving with Focus. And if you bung up something or someone, you'll organize payments, any insurance stuff, and any traffic tickets and all their costs. If you want independence, you get full independence…both the good and the bad-assed parts of it." Both men showed a little surprise at the voice and vocabulary Becky was slipping into.

She looked questioningly at Howard. He nodded "Yes" in body language. The daughter turned and went down the hall and returned in 20 seconds. At the kitchen doorway, she extended her arm with a set of keys strung on a small blue wire cable.

"Dad, take these if you must. Howard and I have only been looking out…"

Her father interrupted. "No more words, Becky. We've all said way more than enough words." Jake took the keys and walked toward the basement door. With his hand on the knob, he turned and was about to speak when Howard spoke one last time.

"Jake, You're right. No more words. Don't drive stupid. Enjoy your beer. Drink in your independence…and we'll enjoy ours. G'night." He put his arm around Becky with his hand on her buns, leading her down the hall toward their bedroom.

Audition
by Susannah Albert-Chandhok

Stealing the key was simple. Scaling the chain-link fence would be more difficult.

Their high school lay contiguous to the town's main road, so the pair had to wait for an atramentous opportunity at night to stealthily propel their bodies forward and upward. Rose struggled to climb, her knee still recuperating from its tear. Peter, with his nimble body, had already reached the fence's apex. He looked down to Rose, bent his torso, and lifted her up and over.

They landed amidst the prickly grass on the other side and panted, from exertion and emotion. While they recovered, Peter glided his hand, like a wave uncovering a creamy seashell in the sand, across Rose's face. His motion revealed hazel eyes beneath a thousand spiral strands of caramel blonde. Her eyes were scintillating, and Peter realized this was due to headlights illuminating them. Silently, he motioned with two fingers for Rose to roll like in the fire safety demonstrations they learned in school.

The pair spiraled and crawled to the space underneath the bleachers, evading capture. They hunched under the incline and regarded each other in the flickering light emanating from the road. Each was covered in crumbs of grass, stubble from the dirt, and concrete debris, all of which stuck resolutely to their salty foreheads and arms. Peter reached out his hand, crocheted with scrapes, to Rose, and she mirrored his gesture without hesitation.

The couple surreptitiously scampered out from underneath the bleachers and across the school's courtyard, which was perpetually under construction. They arrived in front of the door to the auditorium and flung their free hands upon it as if the door was the base in tag.

Peter dug a hand into his denim pocket and found, buried beneath gum wrappers and clinking quarters, a small copper key. He smiled mischievously at Rose. She returned his gaze by biting the corner of her lip. Peter responded with an insouciant head nod as he turned the key, resulting in a reverberating *clink* across the courtyard. They entered.

The beauty of the stillness catches you when you witness an empty auditorium at night. You shiver because the starry footlights make you feel spectral. You feel the presence of innumerable apparitions, and your body undulates to an inaudible pulsation of their whispers, laughter, tears, and applause.

Peter and Rose floated in and out of the rows, mesmerized by the aura of the auditorium and savoring the secrecy of sneaking in. Suddenly, with sideways glances at one another, their dual hypnoses halted. They sprinted to the stage. Despite her recovering knee, Rose arrived first and made her stand firmly at center stage. Peter, arriving a beat later, grabbed her waist and spun her around. Their giggles would stay forever as spirits in the auditorium.

Peter released Rose and faced the audience, opening his arms wide like a composer. He turned back and spoke a wordless directive to Rose's brown-green eyes. Receiving his message, Rose turned away, shaking her head and rubbing her leg. But Peter moved instantaneously and hugged Rose tight, expelling the anguish from her body. Then, he genuflected and kissed her knee.

Rose, galvanized by Peter's adoration and his audacity in stealing the key, nodded.

Peter left the stage and sat in the middle seat of the third row, where he always sat during morning assembly. Rose looked at him one last time from the stage, and then turned her body to face the back. The thousands of specters and the sole spectator simultaneously inhaled.

Rose's right shoulder fell as her right foot pointed and swooped clockwise. Her left foot followed. Now facing the audience, Rose burst open like a lotus and allowed her fingers to float to the heavens as the arches of her feet lifted her up. Seamlessly, she relaxed her appendages and succumbed to melting across the stage, leaving a buttery golden glow in her wake.

Her body moved across the stage with such precision and elegance that Peter didn't need music to make sense of her performance. Rose had learned this piece with her school's dance troupe, but she elaborated upon the movements, infusing them with tenderness, perfecting them.

Mid-dance, Rose attempted a jeté entrelacé, but without the stability in her knee, she stumbled. Peter tensed with solicitude, yet Rose persevered. Improvising now, she ran forward, her toes barely touching the ground as if she was about to launch into the sky, and then she fell, a twirl catching her as she made contact with the ground. Through this blur of motion, Peter noticed her eyes water. Yet Rose's sorrow only fueled her. Each extension of her arm was a dying soldier begging for water and each spin was a child lost within the oppressive canopy of the woods. Despite her emotion, as Rose made her final motion, her visage was unyielding.

The spirits held their applause so that Rose could comprehend the full intensity of Peter's clapping. He climbed over the seats toward the base of the stage and offered her an invisible bouquet. She accepted it and took a final ballerina bow. She swung her legs over the edge of the warm wooden floor and leaped down. Hand-in-hand, Peter and Rose ran up the aisles of the auditorium, the shadows showering them with dandelion seeds, rose petals, and stardust.

They stepped outside into the warm May air, and Peter locked the auditorium door behind them. He faced Rose and again swept away her sticky hair from her face. Her cheeks flushed with the dual vitality of romantic love and inspiration. Peter lay Rose's hand flat against his own and pressed the copper key into her palm. Rose's fingers folded in a nyctinastic motion, treasuring and protecting this gift. As she moved, two wedding rings, which left fresh indentation marks in their skin, clinked.

Behind the Wire
by Hope Longview

"Siri, text David."

"Ok, what do you want to say to David?"

"Cleared customs. Will email about Scotland ASAP. Short version, Pauline's a wreck. Such a sad state. Don't pester me to come home. I'm excited and feel fine. It's been a year. I have to work. Need to work. Gotta run. Love you."

"Ready to send it?"

"Yes."

Suzanne zipped her iPhone into the lining pocket of her Eddie Bauer jacket while scanning for a driver holding up her name. A short blonde wearing threadbare red TOMS bounced on tiptoes and waggled her ponytail.

"Welcome to Greece, Dr. Milton. I'm Jessica Saunders, director of volunteer relations. I'm also your new roommate. Nice trip from Scotland?"

"Call me Suzanne. It was a lot easier than flying from New York. I wanted to visit Pauline. She's had it rougher than most survivors, you know."

"Oh, I didn't realize. Was she in the hospital bombing in Afghanistan or the suicide bombing?"

"Neither. The Save the Children treatment center in Sierra Leone."

Jessica was sleep deprived and hopped-up on bad coffee. She'd been assisting refugees fleeing from ISIS for nearly a year. Recently, the chaos had been unrelenting. But, she wasn't about to admit she didn't know what had happened in Sierra Leone. An earthquake? Flooding? Civil war? Hyper-efficiency was her best shame-control strategy. Without missing a beat, she changed the subject, "Here's your schedule and room key. I'll trade them for your valuables."

Suzanne handed over her passport, cash, credit cards and return tickets as she buckled into the unmarked white van. "I read your security policy. Is that really necessary?"

"Absolutely, the black market is crazier than ever. Remember, no jewelry. Ever. And, electronics remain locked in our room safe. One person's foolishness turns all of us into targets."

~*~

"Here we are." Jessica gestured at the refugee center's main security gate.

Startled, Suzanne realized she had been dozing off for much of the drive. "Uh, why the double fence and razor wire? Do the refugees try to run?"

"No, the razor wire faces outward to keep traffickers from kidnapping women and kids."

"Seriously?"

"Yeah, it's sad. We still lose some teens who sneak out looking for the discos. Some Greek authorities take bribes. Look the other way."

"What happens to the girls that get taken?"

"Guys and girls. They're smuggled off to brothels and slavery. Or, they're sold to ISIS and radicalized or forced into 'suicide' bombing. Their families are forced to move on without them. I've never heard of any being recovered.

"Let's drop your stuff off in our room and I'll show you around before we head to Rainbow Center."

"Sure. It won't take two seconds to change into scrubs so I can start seeing patients."

"Relax. No need for scrubs today."

"You don't have to coddle me. I'm ready to jump in."

"Way above my paygrade. Schedule's set by Director Harris."

~*~

Director Harris hired Suzanne to run the Rainbow Center, a thirty bed Pediatrics ward within the larger infirmary. Overseeing such a small unit should be a cake walk for her. She wondered what their main diagnoses would be. But, none of the kids appeared to be ill or receiving medication. As she spent the balance of the morning meeting the staff and kids, she kept asking to see their charts but was told there would have plenty of time for that after lunch. Two hours later she was getting weary and chided herself for laying around too much while back home. One of the volunteers even made her sit down and offered her a bottled water, "Jetlag and the heat can really suck the energy out of you."

Jessica escorted her to lunch where they joined a noisy table of gals in the back corner. "Dr. Milton, let me introduce you to the rest of Rainbow Team."

"Nice to meet you. I'm a Med Peds doctor from Manhattan. I've spent the last 20 years doing relief work all over the world. Tell me about yourselves." They went around the table telling their stories. Suzanne noted there were a dozen gals with eight more on duty on the ward. Their average age couldn't be more than 25. None of them, except Jessica, had been at the relief center more than 2 weeks and she was the only one planning to stay more than a month. A couple of them were nurses but most of them were teachers and other non-medical volunteers. She wondered how she was going to run even a small Peds ward around-the-clock with almost no medical staff.

"Dr. Milton, er…Suzanne, sorry to cut short your lunch. It's time for your intake meeting with Director Harris. Feel free to bring your tray." Jessica stood gesturing toward the exit.

"No need. I'm finished."

Director Harris welcomed Suzanne into his spartan office. "Thanks for joining our team. We sure need the help. Now, I know you could run this whole shebang so don't be shy 'bout telling me what I'm doing wrong." His Texas drawl put her at ease. "The kiddos aren't sick. They're in lockup because they've gotten lost from their families in the chaos of landing on the beaches. Most probably aren't orphans or intentionally abandoned. We take their photos, try to get their names, estimate their ages. If we're lucky their families write a name, birthdate, and a cell phone number on their back or belly with waterproof marker. Those kids are usually easy. Most of those get reunited with family in the first four days of arrival."

"What happens to the rest?"

"They stay with us for thirty days. Then they're transferred to an orphanage in Athens. From there, who knows. These kids aren't eligible for adoption and they may never be unless the UN and EU can decide how to resolve their cases."

"Ok. So Rainbow ward is about comfort measures until family arrives or they are transferred out. Anything else?"

"Don't get attached. They'll break your heart. More than half of your work will be to keep your volunteers going. Most of them leave early because they can't take the sadness anymore."

The rest of their meeting was matter-of-fact. "There are 5 new kids coming in from the beaches. They are all marked—three brothers, two cousins. Parents will be cleared to pick them up by tomorrow afternoon. Jessica will explain the release protocol to you."

~*~

Suzanne was proud of herself for not losing it when faced with running a whole unit of lost children. She was managing well until the smaller of the new brothers climbed onto her lap sobbing. As she rocked him to sleep, she couldn't keep from crying but hoped none of her volunteers noticed.

Later that evening, Jessica walked in as Suzanne sat silently sobbing. She shoved the crisp new American passport into her pocket. "Oh. Sorry. Didn't mean to startle you," Jessica apologized. "You know all passports have to be locked up, right?"

"It's not my passport." Suzanne handed it to Jessica pointing to the photo. "His name was Suah, it's a Liberian name that means 'a new beginning.' I stayed in Monrovia an extra year to adopt him. One Friday in July of 2014, I went to the US Embassy to have his papers finalized and get his passport. I left him with Charity, his nanny. Her mum came for a visit but didn't tell anyone about the fever she'd had for 3 days. Not that we would have known what it meant. Not at that point anyway. At the bus stop on the way home she collapsed. Two days later she became our hospital's first ebola fatality. Soon, Charity's father and two sisters also died. By the end of the next week Charity and Suah were buried with them and dozens of other ebola victims in a mass grave behind the hospital. Suah was a week short of his 2nd birthday. In mid-October, when my contract ended I was urged to go back to the US. By Halloween, I was at Bellevue Hospital in New York wondering if I was going to die from ebola too. It's been a year. I'm still exhausted and can't seem to quit crying. My brother, David, said I wasn't ready yet. I guess it was a mistake to come here. Director Harris will probably send me packing. He doesn't seem to put up with much."

Now, Jessica remembered what had happened in Sierra Leone. Pauline was the Scottish nurse who had survived ebola. Jessica realized why Harris wanted her to keep an eye on Suzanne. "Does Harris know?"

"Yeah, he knows. He took a risk on me because I've had fewer post-ebola syndrome issues than a lot of survivors. But, I still get fatigued and have muscle pain. But, my eyes are good so far. He knows I have to send my surveillance samples to the CDC via diplomatic pouch while I'm here. But, he's promised not to tell anyone."

"No. I mean does he know about your son?"

"No one knows. Not even my brother. I can't believe I blurted it out to you."

"You haven't told your family?"

"You'd have to know my brother. He thinks humor is the cure for everything and I just couldn't deal with it. He knows I'm sad. But, he thinks I was in love with someone I left behind in Liberia. I guess in a way he's right. Do I have to talk to Harris about it?"

"Your secret's safe with me. But, it's a whopper. I'd encourage you to share it—when you feel able. By the way, the gals on your team love that you cried with that boy this afternoon. Most of them sob into their pillows at night. Seeing you cry on the ward has helped them. Three of them have already extended their stay for another month. And, you've just been here 12 hours. The director won't send you home if I have anything to do with it."

~*~

At 5am the next morning Director Harris knocked on Suzanne and Jessica's door with armed security.

"I hate to alarm y'all so early in the mornin'. But, Suzanne, your friend, Pauline, has been flown from Scotland to London in critical condition. They've confirmed she has ebola reactivation causing meningitis."

"What?"

"I know, it takes a bit to process it. I've been on the phone since

2am and I still can't wrap my head around it. The world didn't even know reactivation was possible—not after 8 months virus free."

"How bad is she? Do they think she's going to make it?"

"I really don't know. But, unfortunately, that's the least of our worries right now. The CDC and EU are coordinating a containment strategy. Their team will arrive this afternoon."

"Oh, sure. Will they call to give us updates on her?"

"I don't think you understand. Their team will arrive *here* this afternoon. Until they clear you of infection, all the rest of us and the whole refugee center are on lockdown."

Burned

by Billie Holladay Skelley

J.T. Hopkins had always wanted to be a fireman. From the first time he held a toy fire engine as a child, he knew it was his calling. As he grew older, it became his passion. Fire held an innate appeal for him. He liked the lights that danced in the flames, the power that radiated from the heat, and the intoxicating smell of the fumes that hinted at both excitement and danger. Every part of the job captivated him.

Civic duty, of course, was also important to J.T. He believed in the rural tenet of serving your community and giving back to the folks who have helped you. In church, they always preached about treating people the way you want to be treated, and he thought it was a good philosophy. Respect relationships and be kind to your fellow man was his motto. Besides, in isolated, remote areas, like where he lived, people needed to be good to their neighbors. They had to help each other out, just so everyone could get by.

His favorite part of being a fireman, however, was the camaraderie he shared with his fellow volunteers. He had made many true friends among the crew, like Colt and Mason, but almost all the men were superb people. They were dependable when needed and heroic when required.

Of course, J.T.'s actual path to his chosen profession hadn't been straightforward or simple. Four years ago, when he was only eighteen, he had applied for the open position on the county's volunteer fire department. Chief Randle, the man in charge, had turned him down. The Chief said J.T. was too scrawny, didn't have his own vehicle, and needed to mature. He was devastated at the time, but that was four year ago.

Now, at the mature age of twenty-two, J.T. had filled out considerably, and he owned a Ford F-350 Dually. He'd also settled down and married Mary Louise Carson, the prettiest girl in the county.

When he'd applied again to the fire department last year, Chief Randle couldn't refuse him. Besides, this was no big city department with EMTs, hazmat units, and forensic experts. It was just a rural, volunteer crew composed of neighbors who wanted to help each other.

J.T. had proven himself early on. There had been a barn fire a week after he got the job, and J.T. was the first man there. He saved four horses, and the rancher was so grateful, he made a big donation to the fire department.

During the past twelve months, J.T. had been on many calls. He had shown himself to be dependable, capable of handling the equipment, and able to function even when surrounded by fear. He was worthy of his fellow firemen's trust. J.T., it seemed to everyone, was meant to be a fireman.

One evening, during the early weeks of his second year on the volunteer fire crew, J.T. raced his truck toward the firehouse. His tires were flying across the dirt road and creating a dust storm in his wake. Exceeding the speed limit greatly, he screeched to a stop in the graveled parking lot. Colt and Mason, who were sitting on the firehouse's porch, called to him as he got out of his truck.

"J.T., you drive like a bat out of hell," said Colt. "Where's the fire, man? What's your hurry? We were just wondering where you were."

"Nowhere," answered J.T. "Just hanging out."

"You smell like gasoline," said Mason waving his hand in front of his face.

"I just filled my tank," answered J.T.

Joining them on the porch, he sat down in the remaining chair.

"You know," J.T. added, "I've been thinking. This past year has been so great working with you guys. I've learned so much."

"You're a natural, J.T.," interrupted Colt.

"Thanks, Colt, but I mean it. I'm amazed at how everything can change in just a short period of time and how things still can work out so well."

Suddenly, their phones went off informing them that there was a burning vehicle on Crab Orchard Road. Someone had seen the fire and called it in. Crab Orchard Road wasn't far from the firehouse. They all knew it well. The site was a popular place for the county's young lovers to park and get better acquainted.

"Someone was probably smoking or drinking or both," Mason shouted as he ran toward the department's old fire engine.

"Damned fools probably set themselves on fire."

J.T. and Colt jumped in their vehicles as Mason turned on the siren and sped off. They followed behind him toward Crab Orchard Road. When they arrived, they saw a 2002 Pontiac Firebird engulfed in flames. As the first three responders, they immediately began to reach for their gear in the fire truck.

Suddenly, the gas tank of the Pontiac exploded forcing all three men to seek shelter behind the fire truck. For a moment, the gray evening air was lit up by the flash of the fireball. The gas was quickly consumed, and the three men left their shelter and set about uncoiling the hose from the fire truck. Soon, they were applying the full force of the water held in its tank.

The flames were resilient, however, and suffocating heat continued to emanate from the vehicle. The power of the fire infused through J.T.'s veins and quickened his movements. The danger in front of him was obvious, but he could not deny the excitement that was present also.

More volunteer firemen arrived, and they all began to sense there would be no survivors from this one. Twenty minutes passed before some of the men felt they were actually starting to get the upper hand in this battle with the flames. Finally, the fire was out, but the air remained heavy with the smell of gasoline fumes intermingled with burnt hair, scorched fabric, and charred metal.

Mason went to check out the smoking car, even though he knew there was no hope for its occupants. J. T. began to retract the hose, while Colt tried to control the growing crowd of onlookers.

Colt saw Mason approaching the hot car and yelled to him.

"Be careful. I still smell gasoline...there had to be some sort of accelerant involved before the gas tank went. The flames were too hot, and it burned too fast."

J.T. finished with the hose and began to stow some of their gear in the cabin of the fire truck. Colt, seeing the county sheriff and his deputy arrive, left the crowd control to them and started helping J.T. with the gear.

Suddenly, Mason approached J.T. and Colt. His face was ashen, but not from the fire.

"J.T., it's...it's Mary Louise."

He stretched out his arm and placed a blackened piece of metal into J.T.'s hand.

"That's the barrette she always wore in her hair...and," Mason's voice faltered, "and it's Captain Randle. They're both holding each other in the front seat."

Colt gasped in disbelief.

J.T stared at Mason as if he must be mistaken. His eyes carefully studied the burnt barrette. His hands began to shake. Finally, he glanced toward the scorched vehicle, but his feet did not move toward it. Instead, he hurriedly sought the privacy and safety of his own truck. Laying his head on the steering wheel, he began to sob.

His fellow firemen granted him his space. For them, this was hard to figure. Unfaithfulness was one thing, death was another, but both together were just too much. It was unfathomable. No fire drills or practice routines ever prepare you for something like this. They sensed J.T.'s despair and confusion. Their sorrow for one of their own hung as heavy in the air as the chemical fumes.

Not one of them saw J.T. unlock his glove compartment and take out a photograph of Captain Randle kissing Mary Louise. They didn't see him fold the picture accordion style and clamp it tightly together with the barrette. He was alone and hidden in the truck as he dropped the clamped photo into a rusty gas can containing only half its usual amount of gasoline. Locked away in this destructive chemical bath, the photograph would be erased and forgotten. No key would ever open this container to reveal his secret. It was over. Respecting relationships was still important, but none of the heartache mattered now. It was over.

J.T.'s comrades heard his truck start, and they watched him slowly drive away. Mason, Colt, and the other volunteers knew J.T. must be overcome with emotions. No one wanted to intrude upon his grief. They would comfort him later. Right now, he needed his space. They worried for their friend, but they knew he would be back. J.T. was young, and he would recover. It would take time, of course, but he would return. J.T. was born to be a fireman.

Chokehold
by Diane Siracusa

A brisk wind blew out of the north and Dora watched leaves skitter around and pile up against hedge rows. She turned to sweep the leafy debris out from under her porch furniture and then paused to stare at the house across the street.

Yellow tape blocked the bungalow's front door and even though investigators finished their work days ago, no one came by to remove the conspicuous banner. Instead, it flapped back and forth in the wind and announced what no one wanted to think about: "A horrible crime happened here!"

If someone didn't remove the tape soon, Dora decided she would march over there and take it down herself. She turned to go inside, but stopped to lift her broom in the air and said, "It's the least I can do for you, Beverly!"

No person can escape what life throws at them, but sometimes an individual sets things in motion and bad stuff happen because of it.

On the day of the crime, Beverly woke up early and remained motionless under her bedcovers. Her peripheral vision outlined the barest details of the man next to her. He sprawled across two-thirds of the mattress - like it was his God-given right to invade her side of the bed.

Beverly shut her eyes. She did not have to see Edgar, to know what he looked like. Her husband's hair stuck out at odd angles, stubble covered his bloated face and the sweat-stained tee shirt and shapeless shorts he slept in concealed little of his overweight body.

She opened her eyes again, and only when she knew for certain *he* was still asleep, did Beverly allow herself to slide off the bed and creep into the bathroom. Her hand paused above the doorknob; Beverly knew if she locked the door and Edgar found out, he would break it down. He'd done it before and she suffered the consequences – he beat her, called her names, threw everything out of the cabinet and roared, "Clean up this mess!"

Days later Edgar's brother helped put the door back in place and the pair rewarded themselves with beer, lewd jokes and junk food. They expected Beverly to wait on them and she did so in silence. Afterward, she stood at the kitchen sink and shrank within herself as nauseating cigar smoke fouled the air. Edgar knew his wife hated the smell of cigars and laughed at her obvious discomfort.

Degradation changes a person and the stranger in the bathroom mirror regarded Beverly with disdain. "You're afraid to do anything – you pathetic, stupid woman!"

Beverly cringed; Edgar's words had become her own, but as she looked at the fresh bruises on her arms she whispered the unthinkable, "I wish he was dead!"

Her body tensed up as her mind replayed the previous night's events. She remembered Edgar stuffing his mouth with food and then suddenly gagging. When she asked if he was choking, he nodded, clutched his throat and stood up so fast, his chair fell over. Without hesitating, Beverly ran behind her husband and strained to reach around the bulk of his body until her hands finally met under his rib cage. She pulled back as hard as she could again and again, until the offending piece of food popped out.

Edgar coughed and took a few deep breaths. Then, he whirled around and slapped his wife in the face. She remembered how he squeezed her arms and shook her until she thought her neck would snap. "Stupid, good-for-nothin' woman! Food was too dry and almost killed me!"

Afterward, Beverly cleaned up broken dishes and the food he had thrown on the floor and she wept. "Why did I help him? Next time, I'll just let him be."

Right now, right here in the bathroom, a thought formed in Beverly's mind. "I can make *next* time happen!"

She reached up and pulled open the medicine cabinet. There on the shelf was a box of antihistamine capsules. Beverly knew all about the drug's side effects, but it gave her a sort of grim pleasure to read *dry mouth* on the list. Her husband's gluttonous nature and these pills just might put an end to her miserable life with Edgar. "No one will ever know how it really happened and I will be free!"

Beverly pulled on her bathrobe and dropped eight capsules into the pocket. As she tiptoed into the hallway, her breath came out hard and fast. "You can do this! You can do this! You can do this!"

she repeated over and over as she hurried toward the kitchen.

Terrified by what she was about to do, but determined to go on, Beverly willed herself to start breakfast. The familiar routine and aromas calmed Beverly's growing anxiety and, by the time she heard Edgar stomp his way into the bathroom, her hands were steady enough to break apart four of the capsules. She watched the soft powder disappear into the pot of coffee. "With a little sugar, he won't even know the difference!"

Edgar eventually slouched his way into the kitchen and dropped down onto his chair. He did not look at his wife, but waited for his food in silence. Never sure what might cause Edgar to lash out at her, Beverly put the plates and coffee mugs on the table with great care and said nothing as she sat down.

Edgar looked at his plate of food and said, "This better not be stone cold like yesterday!"

Beverly's body stiffened and she looked down at her plate and waited for him to start eating. Apparently the food suited him because he shoved bacon and eggs into his mouth like a hog at a trough. He took no notice of Beverly's lack of appetite and, after Edgar mopped up the last bit of egg with a piece toast and washed it down with his third cup of coffee, he got up and left the room.

Beverly wanted to jump for joy. Instead, she cleared the table like she always did and, as incongruous as it seemed, prayed for the courage to keep going.

For the rest of the morning, Beverly avoided Edgar and stayed focused on the next phase of her plan. She cleaned the house and prepared lunch with a sense of confidence and by the time she stirred the second dose of antihistamine powder into Edgar's thick, chocolate milkshake, the emboldened woman did so without hesitation. She set the twelve-ounce glass on the table with a thud, "Here you go, Edgar."

Her husband stared at Beverly and she froze in place – her eyes locked onto his. Did the firm tone of her voice just ruin everything? She turned away and walked to the sink. "Please, please, please drink it," she whispered.

Beverly needn't have worried; glutton that he was and mentally dulled by the previous dose of antihistamines, her husband drank the milkshake without saying a word.

This simple plan to rid herself of Edgar moved along with

almost straightforward ease, but even so, Beverly's conscience punished her. One moment she approved her decision to do away with her husband and the next moment she felt like throwing up. In the end anger and loathing won out and she went ahead with phase three of her plan – the last meal.

He will be killing himself she rationalized as, once more, she prepared food for the man who abused her – three thick pork chops – well-done and very dry with a side of mashed potatoes – no gravy. Edgar loved pork chops and Beverly knew he would eat them even if they were as dry as dust.

The man lived by his rules and his routines and at exactly five o'clock, Beverly placed Edgar's dinner on the table. Moments later, he came into the kitchen and sat down with a sullen look on his face. Beverly knew he approved of the meal because he grunted and licked his lips.

Edgar did not even look up when his wife left the room. It was Saturday, the day he allowed her to walk the five blocks to church to attend evening Mass. Beverly's heart raced as she put on her coat, grabbed up her purse and hurried to the front door. Before she left the house, Beverly called out to her husband, "Edgar, don't eat too fast," and in a whisper she added, "You might choke to death!"

Many things had been set in motion that day, but the day was not over, yet. Across the street, Dora stood outside on her front porch and watched Beverly hurry away from her house and down the sidewalk. "Yoo-hoo, Beverly!" she called out.

Beverly did not want to acknowledge Dora; all she wanted was to get away from her life and Edgar. But, Beverly did look back and, in doing so, felt compelled to lift her hand and wave. This simple, human connection derailed everything. Hot tears streamed down Beverly's face, "What have I done?"

By the time the poor woman ran back to the kitchen it was almost too late. The blue color of Edgar's lips told her everything. She ran behind him and, in a nightmarish replay of the previous evening, pulled against his midsection – again and again and again.

Lucky for Edgar, the piece of food finally exploded out of his mouth and, in a state of shock, Beverly watched her husband's face regain its color. As he sucked in air with deep, hoarse gasps, she repeated over and over, "I'm sorry, I'm sorry. I didn't mean it."

Edgar looked at her and rage took over his mind! The man

grabbed Beverly's neck with both hands and he squeezed until she stopped breathing and fell to the floor.

Epilogue:

The police listened to Edgar's explanation of how he thought his "no-good, dead wife" had tried to murder him, but the detectives found no evidence of wrongdoing where she was concerned. He, however, was handcuffed, read his rights and taken away.

Flight in Moonlight
by Susan Koenig

Janine cupped her hand over the phone to prevent the angry voices from drowning her words. "Freda, I'm coming over."

"What's going on?"

"Parental truce failure."

"I'll keep the piano bench warm."

Janine kicked the stand and hopped on her bicycle. The garage door muffled her father's shout, "She'll have a chance to learn from a professional."

She rode through the cool October air to her friend's quiet home one neighborhood away. The garage door stood open and Freda waved her in.

When they practiced together, Freda slid onto the bench first while Janine curled up in an overstuffed chair where she monitored her cell phone. After thirty minutes of required practice, Freda often played things she had been working on by ear. Today, she played "What Now My Love," a song her mother sometimes listened to while reading.

As she struggled to find a note, her father came into the room and pressed a key. She incorporated it. No words were exchanged. Freda's mother stood in the doorway, misty eyed.

"Your turn." Freda hopped up from the piano as calm as if she had been playing chopsticks.

Janine put her sheet music in place and sat erect, wrists hovering, fingers relaxed, mind cluttered with parental barbs. Amid the echoes of their harsh words, she descended into the mechanical execution of notes. She repeated until her thirty minutes ended.

"Bike ride?" she asked Freda.

Their favorite perch was a small hill that overlooked the junior high. They propped their bikes against a tree and sat on the park bench facing the school grounds.

"Tomorrow we get new pieces," Freda said. "I hope Moonlight

Sonata is one of the choices."

"I hate recitals."

"They're not so bad."

"It's what happens afterward at home. 'Too mushy on the arpeggio, not enough staccato in the opening bars, the school needs to hire a piano tuner.'"

Freda didn't respond.

Janine opened her mouth to cry out that her parents were forcing her to move, but the words burned in her heart, trapped.

The following day, Janine waited outside the piano room. When the door opened, Freda emerged flushed with excitement, waving the piece "Moonlight Sonata" above her head.

During Janine's lesson, the piano teacher presented her with "Flight of The Bumblebee."

"Don't I get a choice?"

"Your father called. He was very concerned that the choices weren't challenging enough."

"He called you?"

"Janine, I do think you have the ability to learn this piece. You're very talented. But if you want, I'll come up with several that are equally challenging so you can choose."

"I don't care about that."

"Your father said you're moving to Rhode Island. I didn't know. Have you told your friends?"

"I can't. When I try, it hurts. The words get stuck."

"Have you told your parents how you feel?"

"Why bother? It's like this recital. They control my life." Janine fingered the sketch of a bee on the cover of the piece, wings open and transparent. "But I'll do it. I'll learn it."

Each day, Janine waited while Freda completed her practice after which they swapped places. Once, after they had begun to memorize the pieces, Janine pulled her hands from the keyboard half-way through the first page.

"What's wrong?"

"It's phony. The bee wouldn't be happily buzzing around. It doesn't have feelings. A bee moves on instinct."

"Maybe it's energetic, not happy."

"I don't like it."

"Maybe the bee's purpose is to find honey and it flies frantically, like a trapped bird, until it finally finds a flower at the end of the song."

Janine looked off to the side. Her hands gripped the bench.

"You're right." She sat up straight, positioned her wrists and let her fingers fall into the keys. Aggressive notes emanated from the piano in a wild flight to the chimney and out into the air. Janine's body tensed as she moved through the passages toward the climax. When she finished, she looked at Freda whose mouth hung loose, surprise on her face.

"That was beautiful," Freda's mother said from the arched doorway. Her hands were clasped as if frozen in applause while her fingertips touched her chin.

"Wow," Freda said.

Later, on the hill overlooking the junior high, Janine knew the time had come. She walked toward Freda who was unfastening a water bottle strapped to her bike. As Janine moved, echoes from the morning bout sent a shiver through her.

"If you would just listen," her mother had shouted. "Your daughter is in the middle of a school year in case you hadn't noticed."

"It's the opportunity of a life time. We're going." And then her father had said something that stopped Janine in her tracks. "I'm going and Janine is coming with me. You do what you want."

Janine let the echo die down. Then she said, "Freda, I have something to tell you." Her voice broke.

"What's wrong?"

She trembled as she told her friend everything.

Six weeks later, the recital was held in the school cafeteria. A baby grand, usually pushed into the corner and shrouded in a dust jacket, shimmered with light reflected from its well-polished black finish. The lid stood raised at an angle. Large pots of chrysanthemums from the fifth grade garden decorated the stage and the perimeter of the room. Folding chairs faced the stage. Neat stacks of the evening's program were situated on small tables next to the doors that led to the parking lot.

Students talked nervously behind the large velour curtain that hung from a pole spanning the wide opening between the cafeteria and the school's main hallway. The sound of scooting metal chairs and parental voices grew steadily and overtook the students' nervous chatter.

"Line up now," Ms. Rose instructed her students.

"Here goes," Janine said.

"Good luck," Freda replied.

Ms. Rose introduced each student. When Janine's turn came, she adjusted the cuffs of the white blouse that protruded under the red velvet jacket her mother had picked out for her. They had argued over a skirt versus slacks, and finally her mother relented and Janine's velvet slacks made a brushing sound with each step she took toward the piano. She checked her form as she sat on the bench. Her fingers flew through the notes with the frantic bee, careening to the end without missing a beat or an ounce of zeal. Amid enthusiastic applause, Janine took her bow, placing one foot behind the other and bending slightly as Ms. Rose had instructed. She took a seat in the front row next to the other students who had completed their performances.

When Freda's turn arrived, she crossed the stage and made eye contact briefly with Janine who gave her a thumbs up. She sat on the bench and patted down the folds of her green dress. The mid-length sleeves revealed graceful arms and thin wrists which hovered above the keys allowing her fingers to drape loosely in the pause before playing. The moment of the pause grew, and Janine noticed that Freda's shoulders looked tight, almost frozen. Then Freda pulled her hands down into her lap and folded them. Janine wanted to ask what was wrong. The room was silent. Someone coughed.

Freda raised her arms once again, wrists above the keys. She leaned forward as if encouraging her fingers to do something, but they floated in disorientation. Suddenly she got up and ran off the stage.

The next student played and several more followed. Finally, with only a few performances remaining, Ms. Rose stepped onto the stage and asked everyone to remain quiet. Freda emerged from behind the curtain. She didn't make eye contact with anyone. Her wrists returned to the waiting position above the keys. Her entire body leaned forward and her fingers came down on the opening notes of the Moonlight Sonata. As she moved through the piece, her shoulders seemed to relax. She played without error and near the end, Janine thought she sensed Freda's usual fluid emotion, but when the piece ended, her shoulders tightened and she got up like a robot. She stared at the floor as she took her bow. She sat in the front row and kept her eyes down.

After the last student performed, Ms. Rose beamed. She hugged Freda and said, "I knew you could do it. That was very brave."

Freda's parents rushed to her side and escorted her to the parking lot, safely sandwiching their daughter.

Janine followed. By the time she reached the door and ran outside, Freda had crossed the lot.

"See you tomorrow," she called.

Freda ducked into the car leaving Janine alone on the lot.

Janine sent another urgent text. No response.

More yelling from downstairs. "I have friends here. You don't."

"There's no time. I address my new staff on Monday."

After that, the voices relented in a dramatic pause before the next escalated round.

Janine's phone buzzed. Finally.

"On my way," Freda's text announced.

Janine moved quietly, looking around every turn to avoid the ogres checking the laces of their gloves in their respective corners of the ring.

She slipped out through the garage and past the huge moving van that extended into the street of the quiet neighborhood. She pedaled toward Freda's house. When they met, they rode to the overlook at the junior high.

"What happened last night?" Janine asked. "Are you okay?"

"I had it all memorized but for some reason, I couldn't remember the first note. Ms. Rose said it was stage fright. She sent me to the practice room until I was ready."

"You left so fast when it was over."

Freda shrugged.

"Your parents protect you. They're so cute together. Mine try to kill each other."

"They love you. They just show it differently."

"Don't do that."

"What?"

"You don't know what you're talking about."

"You know they love you."

"Maybe, but they don't love each other." She frowned. "I've got to get back."

They rode to Janine's house.

"I wish you didn't have to go. I don't even know where you'll live."

Janine's mother opened the front door and called out, "Your suitcase is in the trunk of the car if you need it. We're doing a final walk-through. Do you want to come see if you've forgotten anything?"

"No, mom."

Janine's father backed the car out of the garage and pulled up in front of the house. He walked toward them.

"I hope you'll stay in touch with Janine," he said to Freda. He took Janine's bicycle and secured it to the rack attached to the rear of the car, then hurried into the house.

More shouts filtered through the door. "I'm working as fast as I can," and "We're paying the movers for every hour we delay."

Her father stormed back to the car and stood with the driver's door open, one elbow on top of the door and the other on the roof.

Janine's mother emerged with a travel bag and a large purse suspended from her shoulder. She locked the door and walked quickly to the car.

Janine's father called out, "Let's go, Janine. We have a two-day drive ahead. Say your goodbyes."

As the car pulled away from the curb, Janine waved to Freda whose hand was poised like someone taking an oath.

The two-story house overlooked the ocean and for Janine, the hike to the beach had become her favorite escape. One evening her parents took on the surly topic of whether the new school offered the best fit for their impressionable daughter, so she traveled the familiar route to the narrow strip of sand along the shore and was treated to moonlight dancing on the water. She snapped a picture. She searched for the recording she had made at the recital and attached it with the picture to a text, "Makes me think of you."

She sent the message and waited.

Fun on Wall Street
by Von Pittman

As he stepped off the train, Edwin spotted New York's gaudiest tabloids, stacked in adjacent racks, competing to promote maximum panic. "Dow Crashes 504 Points," in a huge font, covered three-quarters of the front page of Rupert Murdoch's *New York Post*. Mort Zuckerman's *Daily News,* shouted "Shock Market," over a picture of a Stock Exchange floor trader in a royal blue blazer, holding one hand in the air and clamping the other over his forehead. Monday, September 15, 2008, had been a bad day on Wall Street. Tuesday, September 16, promised to be as bad, or worse.

"Some people go to Beirut or Kabul on their vacations; we came to Manhattan during a financial meltdown, Edwin said to his wife Candy. "Kabul might have been more fun." He gave the Pakistani inside the newsstand two bucks and took both papers. "Souvenirs."

They walked up the subway station's stairs to the corner of Broad and Wall. Edwin steered Candy into a Dean and Deluca for a latte and an espresso or two while they read the papers. "Desperate times call for strong coffee."

"We've always had great timing, said Candy. "We moved to Washington State just in time for Mt. St. Helen's to dump six inches of volcano ash on our house. And then our place in Davenport was in the wrong spot during the Flood of '93. And of course our only child was here on Nine-Eleven. Now we get to see a stock market panic."

From stools at the window, they could see camera crews and reporters preparing for stand-ups. "Maybe they want some action shots of brokers and traders jumping out of high windows," said Candy.

Edwin turned to page two of the *Post*. "I think that went out with the Crash of '29. Now they just OD on cocaine, I think."

Candy couldn't concentrate on the *Daily News*. "This city really knows how to have a crisis. All those poor people on Sunday night…"

Two nights earlier they had walked by the Lehman Building, on 7th Avenue, just north of Times Square. At 10:00 p.m. it was fully lighted. The two of them watched men and women in casual clothes—shorts, t-shirts, and flip-flops—leaving the building, alone or in pairs. Suddenly *former* Lehman Brothers employees, they carried small items—lamps, cushions, plants, and most often, cardboard boxes. Their "stuff." Many paused briefly to talk with each other. Some hugged.

When Candy and Edwin turned on the 11:00 news that night, they saw recorded interviews of the newly laid-off "financial services professionals," cardboard boxes in hand, as they left the Lehman Building. The few who agreed to talk with the news crews seemed either resigned or dazed. None seemed hopeful; none were visibly angry.

On Monday—day one of the crash—the Dow Jones took a plunge like an Olympic platform diver. Edwin and Candy spent most of the day at the Metropolitan Museum of Art and the Guggenheim. Panic or no panic, the swarms of visitors had long to-do lists and limited time to complete them. With the museums, then tickets for *Spamalot* in the evening, the couple resolutely kept the bad news at bay.

Tuesday morning, in spite of the obvious and pervasive gloom, they decided to go to the Financial District. They had been visiting New York for the last dozen years, in either the fall or spring. Their daughter Shellie had attended the Stern School of Business at New York University, and then moved directly into a public relations firm in Midtown. Candy and Edwin bought a time-share unit near Columbus Circle to use when visiting her.

The Nine-Eleven attack terrified them. While she was at NYU, Shellie had lived in the East Village, near the Financial District. On all their subsequent trips to New York, they visited Ground Zero and stood silently for a few minutes, in sadness and in anger.

Over the years they had first visited the obvious tourist attractions, then the less obvious ones. In recent trips, they had begun seeking out more obscure spots, like the "old" St. Patrick's Cathedral, in Soho, and the Tenement Museum, on Orchard Street.

Edwin had done a little research, then located and photographed the sites of almost a dozen Mafia hits.

If pressed, Edwin and Candy would concede that they were tourists. However, they considered themselves a good deal more sophisticated than the usual run of visitors. Candy, for example, would never have even considered visiting the outdoor set of the *Today* show to gawk at Meredith Vieira and Matt Lauer. "Why, I'd rather die!" she told friends.

After their first half-dozen visits, they started developing their own private game, "puttin' on the Yankees." As Edwin and Candy travelled around the city, from time to time they affected deep southern accents and an elevated "gee whiz" tone of conversation. They liked to make the New Yorkers think they had run into the most credulous, naïve hicks who ever hit town. In actuality, both were college professors. Candy taught statistics at the University of South Carolina-Aiken, while Edwin was a professor of history at Augusta College, just over the state line in Georgia. Both had grown up in California. As a couple, they had lived in the Pacific Northwest and the Midwest before moving to South Carolina. The more pretentious or smug the New Yorker they encountered, the greater their efforts to assume the personas of rubes from the backwoods, amazed at the wonders of Gotham.

Upon leaving the coffee shop, Edwin said, "I'm not sure I want to visit the Financial District again. This crash is no joke. Yesterday was awful; today looks just as bad. It isn't even 10:00 yet, and we've probably lost tens—maybe even hundreds—of thousands of dollars in our retirement accounts. Thank God TIAA-CREF is one of the most conservative funds there is! Its managers have taken a lot of crap for not grabbing at high-growth equities. But that should pay off for us now." After a pause, he added, "I hope."

Candy said, "You can always have fun in New York, even in the Financial District, even during a crisis. Forget about TIAA for a while. Let's enjoy ourselves, like we do on every visit."

Outside on the sidewalk, the fourth estate had arrived in force. Twenty or more television crews lined the two short blocks of Wall Street. But the reporters were having trouble waylaying anyone of importance to interview. Most of the Street's true powers, the people Tom Wolfe had named "the giants of the earth" in his novel, *The*

Bonfire of the Vanities, were either using alleys and rear entrances to avoid the reporters, or brushing past them, avoiding eye contact.

According to the "Style" section of Sunday's *New York Times*, most of the Wall Street grandees had only recently returned from the Hamptons or Nantucket. But today they did not look fresh, energized, or even powerful. The few possibly important figures that Edwin, Candy, and the television crews spotted looked frazzled. The September humidity, and the rocketing stress levels in their brokerages, investment banks, and law firms were taking a severe toll on their two-thousand dollar suits and four-hundred dollar hairstyles.

Today, the Street's "giants" wanted to avoid conversations with CNBC's "Money Honey," Maria Bartisimo, and its "Street Sweetie," Erin Burnett. Nobody wanted to appear in *Squawk on the Street* sound bites. Today, the giants of the earth were determined not to allow CNN's Lou Dobbs or Fox's Neil Cavuto to glibly comment on their "gloom" or "fright."

As Candy and Edwin walked up Wall toward Broadway, a young man with a microphone approached them. "Sir, are you from out of town?"

"Shore am," Edwin said. He resisted the urge to ask who else but a tourist would be on Wall Street in shorts, sandals, and a University of South Carolina Gamecocks polo shirt. While Candy was more upscale in designer jeans and a green sleeveless blouse, nobody would pick her as a broker, banker, or lawyer either.

"Could I interview you two?" the reporter said, gesturing toward his crew.

"Well, shore," Edwin said. "What station do you boys work for?" Candy reached into her purse for a comb.

"We're from New York 1, a local 24-hour cable news channel." He raised his microphone to about a foot from their mouths. "Where are you two from?"

"Aiken. A little bitty town in South Carolina," Edwin said.

Candy chimed in, "We came up to see the sights. Like the Statue of Liberty and the Empire State Building? Tonight we're going to see *Mama Mia*, you know, on Broadway?" She affected the habit of many southern women, ending sentences with question marks. "And tomorrow morning we're going to Rockefeller Plaza to see the folks on the *Today* show, when they come outside?

We've even made us a little 'Aiken, South Carolina' sign." The reporter got down to business. "Have you heard about the big trouble on Wall Street?"

Edwin held up his *New York Post*. "Indeed we have."

"President Bush says the economy of the United States is fundamentally sound," said New York 1. "Do you find that reassuring?"

Edwin looked straight into the camera lens, assumed his most portentous classroom manner, and said, "That's exactly what President Hoover said back in 1929. And of course it wasn't true. But still, it was probably the right thing to say. Proclaiming that the economy was collapsing would only have spread the panic faster and made things even worse." He added some gratuitous comments about Hoover being a true tragic figure, and ended by saying, "Did you know he lived out his last years right here in Manhattan, in the Waldorf Astoria?"

New York 1 turned to Candy, "What about you, Ma'am?"

"I told my Sunday school class back in Aiken that the rich would have to pay for their sins, 'for it is easier for a camel to pass through the eye of a needle than for a rich man to enter the Kingdom of Heaven,' the Bible says."

The reporter realized that he had found some comic relief on a grim day. "Does this financial trouble cause you to worry about visiting New York? Will you be more cautious about how much you spend while you are here?"

"We're pretty careful anyhow," Edwin said.

"You won't find us eating at Elaine's or the Russian Tea Room, or any of those places you read about in *People Magazine*," Candy said. "TGI Friday or the Red Lobster are plenty good enough for our 35th wedding anniversary tomorrow night. Did you know that the world's largest TGI Friday's is right here in New York, on Times Square? No reservations required?"

The reporter knew he had recorded well beyond thirty seconds. "I hope you two will enjoy your anniversary celebration, and the rest of your visit." He looked directly into the camera. "This is Lewis Frazier, New York 1, reporting from Wall Street."

"Do you think your station will use this?" Edwin said.

"Oh yes. If you can get back to your hotel room, it should be on in about thirty minutes. We'll probably show it three or four times, maybe more."

"Our daughter will be so proud!" said Candy.

Edwin and Candy practically skipped across Broadway. They held their laughter down to snickers until they reached the foot of the steps up to Trinity Church, where they let loose and howled. Candy snorted and said, "You old goat! Lecturing a twenty-year-old about Herbert Hoover! That kid has never even *heard* of President Hoover. He probably hasn't even heard of Bill Clinton."

Edwin collapsed against the wall at the base of the churchyard. "Red Lobster! Our anniversary at TGI Friday's!" He slapped at the stairway wall. "Your Sunday School class?"

Candy, held both hands over her abdomen and shrieked, "Why SHORE!"

Even on a bad day, it is possible to have fun in the Big Apple.

Goodwill

by Andrea Lawless

"Jesus. It hurts."

I turn toward the source of the distress to find that the woman in line behind me is now very much beside me. Her words hang there for a moment before dropping limply to the floor.

Oh, god. Was she—? She wasn't talking to me, was she?

As if in answer to my question she looks at me and says, "My eye. I got a splinter in it."

The woman looks to be in her mid-fifties and has course, cropped hair dyed a brassy blonde. She's thin. Her rouged cheeks have begun to sag into the jowls along her jaw line. Behind her large wire-rimmed glasses with the decorative metal arms her right eye does, in fact, look mean and red. The cheek around it is inflamed and a fat, pink circle surrounds her eye like a target. She holds a CD and a pair of pink tennis shoes clutched to her chest. More words tumble out of her mouth.

"I went to the ER last night. They said it was deep. Sure hurts."

"C'mon, honey, hurry up," she mutters to the clerk under her breath. "I need to get some medicine for it," she explains to me.

I smile briefly and slide a half step forward.

One of the clerks behind the counter picks up a service phone and the din of the store is interrupted by a disembodied voice echoing over the clattering chatter.

"Associate to the registers, please. Associate to the registers."

A clerk is belched out of the belly of the store and walks purposefully toward the counter.

"Oh, good. They're gonna open another register," eye lady observes. "Hey, honey!" she calls to the new arrival. "How you doin'? Got you workin' again, huh?"

"Yep! Can't seem to get away."

She's very pleasant, this new clerk. She punches some keys on the register. "I can take the next person in line," she says, looking at the man in front of me.

"She's good," eye lady says to me. "*Real* good. And fast."

Not wanting to be entirely rude, I give her a feeble smile and exhale a quick burst of air in a polite sort of chortle. A mistake, it turns out.

"Just look at these shoes!" she coos, pulling a tennis shoe away from her chest. She displays it proudly, turning it this way and that to make sure I can see its neon pink glory from every angle. "Four bucks! Like new. Nikes ain't cheap, neither. I grabbed 'em, said, 'Those are *mine*!'" She smiles gleefully at her treasure.

There are only two people ahead of us, but the line doesn't move. The woman just ahead of me at the first register has a full shopping cart and is lifting out every piece she has one at a time, holding it up and examining it carefully before gently laying it on the counter for the clerk to ring up. The new clerk at the far register is still helping the same guy who was next in line even though he doesn't have much. A return, I surmise.

"Brown Eyed Girl!" eye lady spits up onto the CD she is holding. "That's a good one! An oldie. I love that song. It's for karaoke," she says, waving the CD toward me. "I got one a' those machines. The girls love it. They're on it all the time. Love to hear my kids and grandkids sing on it." She has the uninhibited friendliness of someone who is unbalanced or slightly drunk.

"Hurry up, now," she mutters toward the front of the line. "I want to go home." To me she adds, "I got to get my medicine first. I'm not supposed to drive, though." She pulls her shoulder up to indicate her eye. "Can't see out of it." She gives me a conspiratorial smile. "I got *here* all right, though. I just go slow."

"Come on now," she pipes up again toward the registers. "I need to go home."

She shifts her weight from one foot to the other, whether from discomfort or impatience I can't tell. She moves constantly. Small, quick movements like a hummingbird, or someone who's done a couple lines. Ah. I'm on to something, I think. Meth, maybe? Missouri's famous for it. New meth labs are discovered all the time. I steal a peek at her teeth, but they look normal: all there, not brown.

I look in my cart, which has about eight items, and glance over at her two items. The woman is in obvious pain—let her go first, I tell myself. It's not an altogether altruistic thought—letting her go first will get her away from me. And yet, I can't. I can't bring myself to let her go in front of me. I'm put out by this overly talkative, less fortunate soul. But, why? Where's my empathy? I sift through my offended emotions searching for an explanation and I discover I am not as heartless as I feared. My survival instincts have been tapped is all. My reptilian brain has determined that this woman is an obnoxious nuisance, a threat to the tribe. Also, my Spidey sense is tingling. I suspect she is not simply the talkative type with a faulty internal dialogue switch, but is baiting me to let her go first. I am repulsed by her invasive, weed-like personality and pissed at her obvious manipulation.

"Hi, Laura! How's your father?" she asks someone in the line across from us.

"Good. He's good. Home now, thanks," says Laura.

"Well. You tell him I said hi."

"I will." I notice Laura doesn't pursue the conversation. I also notice the new cashier is finishing up with the return at the far register. I turn to eye lady and smile charitably.

"Ma'am? You can go ahead of me."

She doesn't bother to say thanks, just skitters up to the register like a puppy racing toward a bowl of food. My feelings soften to something more like sympathy as I watch her being rung up. I think how painful it must be getting a splinter in your eye, and then I wonder how something like that even happens.

Hanging by a Thread
by Maril Crabtree

Think of a moment in your life when suddenly you can almost see how things flow into one another, almost hear the whisper of the shuttle moving back and forth through the loom; and even though you are consigned to the back side of the tapestry – the side where threads hang willy-nilly, where colors collide in seeming confusion – you glimpse for a split-second the pattern on the other side and feel a deep knowing of how everything fits together. In that rarest of moments, I have found myself saying, as if in prayer, "I could die right now."

The night before my wedding I said these words. I may even have said them out loud.

It was late August, 1962. After the wedding rehearsal, after my husband-to-be and I sweated our way down the maroon-carpeted aisle of my suburban church and plodded through who-takes-whose-hand-when and what-to-do-with-the-veil and the impossibly long satin train of my borrowed wedding dress, we burst into the night like overripe watermelons, anxious to escape and spread our juices everywhere.

It had been an unusually steamy week, even for New Orleans. Jim and I had been apart all summer, he in a Western Kansas grain elevator and I in a vast pool of insurance company secretaries, both of us working diligently to save money for the wedding and graduate school. We'd met in college, a Midwestern school where I'd traded a lush landscape of magnolias, swamps, and Spanish moss for one of sunflowers, wheat fields, and stately oaks.

I'd been less successful at trading a constraining culture of racial segregation for a slightly more enlightened landscape of integration, but at least I'd found partial success. The boy I fell in love with and would now marry was as eager as I to liberalize civilization in the coming decades. The 60's had not yet shattered the world, but I longed for someone clear and charismatic to lovingly place a hammer in my hands.

The wedding party – bride, groom, and four college-age attendants - gathered at a friend's French Quarter apartment for a combined bachelor/bachelorette last fling. *Laissez les bon temps rouler! Let the good times roll!* Our host urged all sorts of exotic goodies upon us, most of which I'd never tasted before: Russian caviar, Brie, anchovies, smoked salmon, German beer and a case – an entire case - of French champagne.

The French Quarter itself seemed magical that night: sounds of Dixieland jazz and late-summer cicadas and distant tugboat foghorns competed with laughter from those lurching in and out of bars on the street two stories below; smells of gardenia and honeysuckle from the courtyard mingled with those of fried oysters and catfish. This was New Orleans at its finest, this cacophony of smells, sounds, sights all blooming up like spring weeds along a forgotten two-lane highway.

A couple of hours later, I left my fellow revelers in the living room and wandered onto the balcony. I wanted to dive into this night. Every square inch of existence embraced me, called me. In a champagne haze I leaned over the dancing wrought-iron railing and stood on tiptoe. The top half of my body jack-knifed over the blurred rail.

As I hung there upside down, blood rushing to my head, I considered, at that moment of half-drunken delirium, whether now – NOW – was the perfect time to die, to literally jump from that balcony into the waiting arms of the gritty bricks and glittering moonlight, to leave this world before I would, the next day, leave behind a part of my singular existence to merge with someone else's. In the pure, aching bliss of that moment, I glimpsed the other side of that mystery-laden cosmic tapestry, felt the patterns of my own life shift irrevocably.

Then I felt my beloved's arms around my waist, pulling me gently away from those other waiting arms, pulling me back into ordinary time and space. The impulse vanished as swiftly as a summer rain.

"Come back inside. There's coffee and Kahlua," he said. "Good thing you came out for some air. Dave puked all over the bathroom rug."

Next morning, I awoke with a slight headache, a pounding heart, and a whole lifetime still ahead of me, a lifetime in which the patterns sometimes looked as strange to me as a foreign land. I willingly bonded with another, but at times fought to keep my soul *and* my body independent.

Fortunately, I married someone who understood that marriage itself did not guarantee him any "rights" to either. I have found that within the "bondage" of relationship there is an opportunity for both partners to weave their side of the tapestry into something beautiful and lasting.

All it takes is a certain kind of fidelity that people often omit from their commitment vows: fidelity to oneself and one's own truth, even if that truth is elusive, hidden, and ever-changing. If both partners have a sense of that fidelity, marriage becomes an open door, an invitation to explore life from within the mutually constructed haven of love and respect.

Of course, I didn't know any of that when I leaned over the balcony that night, nor for quite a few years thereafter, but I learned, he learned, and we shared what we learned. Our mistakes became part of the pattern, with their own peculiar beauty.

Two children, four grandchildren, five careers, and 53 years later, we're still weaving patterns, individually and together. Sometimes we still don't see how they fit into the whole tapestry, but we've learned to trust each thread for its unique contribution. Time itself has a way of disappearing as we've learned to cherish the moments. Every now and then, I feel that dizzying instant when the veil seems to part and life/death seems poised to surrender to something wonderful and immense. But I also still have that feeling of a whole lifetime ahead of me – knowing that a lifetime includes whatever comes next, with a partner who'll hold my hand along the way.

The Incident at Bleeding Creek Trestle
by Pablo Baum

Carlie knew that double tracked trestle, she just didn't know what awaited it. No one did. No one could. She had climbed it uncountable times during her ten years of life as an only child, and she knew how it creaked and complained as the heavy trains traversed its spans, high overhead, sometimes two at the same time chugging along in opposite directions, while engineers waived at little Carlie far below.

As Bleeding Creek flowed below, it refreshed and elated her in the hot summers as its soft mud oozed between her toes and she would laugh.

The towering Father Oak, the largest known to man—or child—was her most revered and preferred of all, for it embraced her and protected her in its velvety shade so that they, together, could unite and languish in such serene sanctuary. They were all companions in this special place of the backwoods: a trestle, a creek, an oak, a child.

Carlie's dark-brown, straight hair reached her waist and always had, whether in pigtails, pony tail or flowing freely in the breeze, she rhymed her Cherokee mother's femininity and her father's gray-blue Germanic eyes. He had been a valued engineer on the trains, but, before Carlie's birth, he had become a soldier who never returned from a place called Shiloh back in 1863. Her mother's wondrous stories of him stirred Carlie to attend with reverence her precious retreat of Bleeding Creek and to lift her eyes in awe at that verdant grandness that promised to embrace and shield her with downy fondness always.

Carlie lived with her frail mother near the trestle. Before the horrific news from Shiloh she had been a vibrant woman, but now the skin beneath her eyes sagged heavily, and her sunken cheeks, her bony shoulders and fingers along with nearly snow-white hair, made her older than her years. But the two, lovingly loyal, managed to survive from their gardens and what they could sell when compassionate engineers, who had known her father, would stop their trains and permit passengers to purchase what they wished. Life, Carlie's mother knew, was grim, but at least the foolish war was long over.

November came, cold and dark, and the rain announced itself that evening by gentle drizzle that awakened neither mother nor daughter. Wind. The house creaked. Windows rattled. They awoke. Cold, searching and malevolent, slinked through hair-line breaches like myriad scorpions bent on torment once inside. The stone fireplace had gone dark, its flames from earlier that calm evening now nearly extinguished. Draping blankets over their heads, clutching them tight under their chins, they shivered before the dank hearth. Carlie, as was her usual task, re-kindled and re-fueled its flames as the wind and vicious down-pour burst into something greater, ripping shingles one by one, allowing icy water to flow through first one breach, then another, splashing, pooling on the compacted dirt floor.

Together, embracing, they shuddered as the straight-line wind growled and snarled, the watery roar of nearby Bleeding Creek adding to the din. Even the nascent flames seemed to cow against their frigid foe casting a feeble glow on the two tense faces, faces of defenseless ones who clutched each other, intertwined, becoming one, while Mother hummed the old Cherokee lullaby with which *her* mother had reassured her cherished brood that dangers of the elements could not harm them, that the bearded ones could not deprive them of their home, could not leave them in the cold, that this night's storm, or ogres' harm, would not destroy their humble haven, dared not leave them there alone.

Then came a rattling, rhythmic clacking, that clamorous clatter of the midnight train that advanced toward Carlie's trestle, the trestle she knew was weakened by such trials yet unknown.

"Mother, Mother … the engineer … there is no way that he can know." Then: crashing, crumbling timbers accompanied by a mashing of metallic mayhem.

Carlie pondered it for not more than the blink of an eye, for she knew a second train was coming, a *passenger* train, within the hour. Seizing her coat of many colors from the hook near the door, and donning flimsy moccasins, she stepped out despite the desperate protests of her mother who lacked the strength in her failing body to thwart her beloved's daring departure. The dogged head-wind tumbled her back against the closed door, but leaning forward at the waist, she pushed against her adversary, glancing up into the darkness that allowed her only glimpses of its mysteries, bursts and flashes.

The rail fence. The fence her father had built, anchoring it to that oak tree far, so very far down the path at the creek bank. Gripping the top rail, placing one gloveless hand over the other, one foot before the other she pulled herself toward the trestle. The rumble of the swollen creek colliding against wood and metal increased as she neared. On she went. The freezing blasts into her face numbed her, soaked her, her lashes sagged under flecks of ice that glistened in the abrupt illuminations, but stop she would not.

Father Oak. That centennial giant that she had climbed upon and napped under, the sage that had offered its hospitality to an aviary of life and color for longer than the lives of a thousand creatures, stood in wait of its diminutive daughter, like it always had, inclemency be-damned. She reached her hand through the gloom and it was there. She steadied herself.

The sound and spray of heartbreak needed no lightning's flash to verify its horror. "Can someone hear me?" she shouted, her high pitched voice contrasting with the deep-toned rumble a mere stone's throw away. A pause. Nothing. Then …

"Two dead!" came a man's unsteady voice from amid the tangle.

"Hold on!" she shouted, but then wondered, *now what?*

She felt herself moving, falling. Vertigo? *No*. Her defender, Father Oak—on which she leaned this final time—who had held the sky above, was now assaulted by a tempest, as great as any Shiloh, or flood of Noah's time, could now endure no more. The muddy bank had washed away exposing roots, roots larger than many trees. The giant that had seen the coming and going of spear toting hunters, the arrival of bearded bearers of bayonets on their cannon laden trains that traversed its companion the trestle, now continued its relentless tilting toward the other side of Bleeding Creek, its splendid mass groaning and creaking and weeping as it slipped from Carlie's tiny hand, then crashing—a thud that surpassed the thunder and the fury of the powers great and dreadful.

Dropping to her knees, she paused, her icy lashes laboring to blink just one more time. Glazed, surreal in the flashes, she regained her composure, her mind returning to the task at hand: *that second train is coming from the opposite direction!*

The wind lessened, the lightning faded and the thunder, so bested by the crash of the noble goliath, departed in shame and Carlie concluded that such improving conditions might embolden the engineer of the coming passenger train to press on and that all would be fine and fitting and secure.

All was not fine, and only two souls in all Creation knew this: slightest Carlie and the desperate survivor who still held onto the wreckage in Bleeding Creek.

She groped her way forward, slithering through the muddy root mass and onto the trunk which she attempted to straddle, as if sitting the saddle of some great percheron, leaning onto her palms, inching her way toward the other side, the raging water close below, the seemingly accidental bridge was solid.

Reaching the first branches, branches she knew as well as did any robin or jay, she schemed around each, using it for firmer grip. Then, she heard that the water was *behind* her. She had made it. Descending to the mud below she felt her way through thickets and brambles toward a place between the rails she knew so well, and firmly in control, she accelerated to a trot, then to a sprint, following the curve, hurling herself through the night under the clearing sky above and the sliver moon that barely lit her way toward old Mr. Elwood's cabin, a mile ahead, where she would secure his red tinted lantern for which any engineer would be compelled to stop.

The air remained cold, but she felt only duty, for the deceptive calm would surely lure the coming souls around that curve, through the darkness and irreversibly onto the yawning portal into perdition.

Far ahead, a tiny light: the train! Would she reach Mr. Elwood's cabin *before* or *after* the speeding train passed? Faster. She must. In the dark, to her right, the cabin! She dashed toward it, through bushes, stumbling, recovering and screaming, "Mr. Elwood" until she reached the door that rattled noisily from the pounding of her little fists, "Mr. Elwood, hand me your red lantern!"

In a moment the door squeaked open and a groggy man with gray, uncombed hair appeared with the lantern already lit, which she seized then sprinted toward the tracks with the agility of a cottontail. The sound and smell of the oncoming train was nearly upon her as she swung the traditional signal of impending crisis. As it passed, slowing, the train's reflective lantern illuminated her face, her tangled icy hair, her muddied coat of many colors, as the screeching brakes protested. The old iron horse stood belching and spewing while dwarfing its commander and her flickering crimson plea.

Old Mr. Elwood, wrapped in the blanket under which he had slept a moment before, now wore his hastily donned boots over bare legs and shivered in the autumn air as he greeted with a bony wave those former colleagues of his younger years. A muscular hand extended down to Carlie, lifting her to join them in the relative warmth of the engineers' lair, crewed by two wise and admiring gentlemen of the rails. The four-car—hitherto doomed—passenger train had been delivered by the slightest of heroines while its puzzled travelers savored sweet salvation.

The plan agreed upon by the experienced engineers under, of course, little Carlie's instructions, was to disconnect the locomotive and tender from the passenger cars—lest the unforeseen imperil its precious human cargo—then proceed to the water's edge and attempt a rescue of the survivor, using ropes and cables of which there were plenty on board.

The sun was rising as they arrived at the muddled mass of wood, metal, water and that majestic oak bridge: a bridge without which Carlie would be observing something quite different from the wrong side of Bleeding Creek. As it was, the victim who had answered her from the gloom of the torrent, emerged broken and icy to begin the first day of the rest of his life.

Carlie, returned that sunny, cold afternoon to the resting place of the one who had guided her … and more. A cardinal came to perch on one of its now vertical branches but did not sing, for it could not know.

But Carlie did.

Inescapable
by Nancy Jo Cegla

Sonny slouched back in his chair with his feet on the porch rail. His ten-gallon hat shaded his closed eyes, but he was not sleeping. He reached into his shirt pocket and pulled another cigarette out and tapped it on the arm of the chair. He lit it with a match scraped across the bottom of his boot, and sucked a deep drag, exhaled with pleasure and a raspy cough. The late afternoon sun filtered through Sycamore leaves cast splotches of light and shadow onto the porch. A small radio played Johnny Cash music.

"Ya smokin' them cigarettes like you all got nine lives."

"Oh, Momma."

"'Oh, Momma,' nothin'. You all know them lungs ain't no good."

"Momma, it's just some smoke wrapped in a piece of paper. Ain't nothin'."

"Ya cheated death once when you was born. It ain't likely ya can do it twice!"

Sonny looked her in the eye and took a deep drag. Momma turned the radio off. Silence settled between them like acoustic tiles absorb sound.

"Heard we got us a new neighbor."

Sonny snuffed out the cigarette on the bottom of his boot tossed it onto the already piled high ashtray.

"Ain't ya gonna ask nothin' 'bout the new neighbor?"

"Weren't plannin' on it. Since ya ask, I spose I'd best be leavin'." He began to unfold himself from the deep angled seat.

"How ya all gonna know 'bout the neighbor if ya be leavin'?"

"Don't want to know."

"Why not?"

"Cause ya asked. Means it's a female."

Momma's face turned sour. She did her best to be coy and smiled sweetly. "Why would ya think that?" A brief silence resumed, "She's purty."

"They always is."

The new neighbor passed along the sidewalk carrying a bag. She moved quickly pulling herself into a slight twist away from the porch as if she would become invisible using the package like camouflage.

"Thar she is now. Hello thar, Missy! Come sit a spell."

Sonny continued to unfold himself into a full stand and turned toward the screen door.

"Sonny, sit down and meet the new neighbor."

"I'm leavin', Momma."

Momma bellowed to the young woman. "Got fresh lemonade. On ice."

The woman politely stopped her escape route to reply, "Thank you. I'd love to stay, but I'm in a hurry."

Sonny tried to escape again. He muttered under his breath, "Run!"

"This here's my boy, Sonny."

"Howdy, ma'am."

The woman turned and walked toward Sonny. She extended her hand, "Hello, I'm—"

"Tall or short glass?"

The woman stopped and looked at Sonny who rolled his eyes. "Really, I must be going."

"Tall it is."

Sonny looked at the young woman and a small grin widened his mouth. He made a sweeping gesture toward an Adirondack chair. She returned his stare in disbelief.

Momma barked, "Sit. Take the load off ya's feet."

Shocked by the volume of the command, the young woman jumped and seated herself to the back of the sloping wooden chair and set her bag down on the porch. "All right, I will."

Sonny interjected a low, but confident voice, "Ya'll be sorry," directed to the woman.

"Not from 'round here, are ya?" Momma said in a friendly voice.

The woman looked at Sonny, hesitated, shrugged and responded, "No. I'm from Minnesota." She, glanced again at Sonny, "Minneapolis, specifically."

"What brings you all this way?"

"Things."

"Thangs? Like what?"

Sonny jumped to the young woman's defense, "Momma, leave her be. Ya don't need to answer. Ain't none of Momma's business. I best be gettin'."

The woman began to slide to the edge of the chair and reached for the bag, "Me, too. I must"

"Drink your lemonade! I mean . . ." Momma's voice turned congenial, "it's a hot one today. Lemonade do ya good. I was just tellin', Sonny here, that he ain't no cat."

"Momma." Sonny moaned with exhaustion.

The young woman looked at Sonny with growing sympathy for Sonny's efforts. "Clearly, he's not. Why did you say that?"

"He smokes them thar cigarettes like he done got hissself nine lives. But he don't. Already used hisself up one, he did. Death his vary self, nearly stole Sonny from his momma before he was ever born."

"Momma. Not that a'gin!"

Momma plowed on, "Sure 'nough did. I was a sleepin', and I done heard a noise, so I sat up and thar he was."

"Who?"

Momma's eyes grew wide, and she stared the young woman in the face, "Death."

"Oh! Look at the time. I really must" and the young woman tried again to unseat herself.

"Sit yaself down a minute, Missy! I's tellin' ya a story. The Grim Reaper, they calls 'em. He tiptoes in, and he grabs a baby out the crib. Poppa and me kept a crib in the bedroom 'cause Sonny was 'bout to be born and all. I miss 'em. My husband that is. Not Death. Seems everybody's a leavin' me sometime."

Sonny mumbled, "Only if they's lucky," and the woman's mouth broke into a slight grin.

"Well, I started to a hollerin'. 'Put that baby down! Get outta here! Shoo!' He stops and stares me right in the eye. Real close like this. And he, gentle like, put that baby down."

"That's . . . quite a story."

"Oh, they's more. Sonny was born to us just a few days later, he was. Early he was. Born with the vary same ailment that

President Kennedy's baby done had."

The young woman looked at Sonny with empathy. "I'm sorry to hear that. It looks like Sonny is fine now."

"Mighty fine now. He's a fighter that one. He done cheated Death . . . that time."

"Momma, people die. It's inescapable. Even the King and Queen died."

"Sonny, that hurts my heart."

"Who?"

Momma and Sonny, with his eyes rolled upwards, simultaneously and enthusiastically responded, "Johnny Cash, and June Carter-Cash."

The young woman looked from one face to the other. She gently and slowly slid her hand to the edge of the arm rests. "Ahhh."

Momma wiped a tear from her cheek. "A sad day. Two sad days. But they's togetha now. I been a thinkin'. I'll bet even St. Peter knowed, Johnny. Johnny'd be a standin' thar with his geetar in one hand, and the other one free to shake St. Peter's hand. 'Hello, I'm Johnny Cash', he'd say. And, June, she'd be thar to take the King's hand and lead him on through them pearly gates."

Quiet ensued as Momma mourned. The young woman reached again for the bag. "That was delicious. Thank you. I must go now. I have to feed Robert."

"Robert? Ya ain't married, are ya?"

"No. Robert is my rat."

At first Momma was relieved that the woman was not married, then she considered what she had heard. "Ya got a rat . . . and ya feed it?"

Sonny attempted to suppress a snort, and Momma flashed a confounded look at him.

The young woman's face opened into an unsuppressed smile. "He's my pet."

A cross between curiosity and hope contorted Momma's face. "Ain't you got nothin' better to love?"

"It's a retired lab rat. I used him in a psychology class. I needed to train him. Behavior modification class."

Sonny asked quietly, "Could ya train, Momma?"

"I heard that, Sonny. Maybe she can train ya . . . to stop that smokin'!"

She shrugged, "I doubt it. I couldn't train my boyfriend, Robert, to stop chasing kittens. Well, that's—"

"You all named your rat after your boyfriend?" Momma considered and added "Rat's don't chase kittens, do they?"

Sonny said, "Wait. Here it comes."

"Oooohhhh."

Sonny took advantage of Momma's nonplussed moment. "I best be gettin'. It's gettin' dark. I'll walk ya down the road." He picked up the bag that the young woman had been carrying. "This must be a five pounder. Mighty hungry rat, ain't he?"

A relieved grin spread across her face and a sparkle brightened her eyes as she looked at Sonny with the understanding that she could only imagine soldiers must feel after winning a battle.

Secrets to a Dead Man
by Brianna Boes

Sometimes the truth is a terrible thing.

"A secret's still a secret if you tell a dead man," Laura would say after telling me the truths she kept hidden from everyone else.

When she was first assigned to care for me, I took in as much as I could when she came to wash my unresponsive body, scrubbing and turning me over and scrubbing me again. Her voice was small and sweet. Her hands calloused at the fingertips. She used her firm, flat middle to aid her in rolling me onto my side. Her perfume was rich and savory; it smelled like the woods in spring. Like fresh air and moss and chopped wood with just a hint of daisies. For a little while, it masked the scent of the hospital. For that reason alone, I loved her.

A guitar player maybe? She seems small, thin. But she's strong for her size, I thought. *She's pretty, I'm sure. Is she a sister? A mother? A lover? Does she read classics?* I loved the classics, and I liked to think she did too.

She was kind to my mother whenever she would visit me. They talked, and eventually Laura would say how handsome she thought I was.

"When he wakes, the ladies will be linin' up for him like *that.*" And she would snap her fingers. My mother would laugh and agree, and I loved Laura for that, too. I rarely heard my mother laugh anymore.

At night I dreamed of her. I didn't know what she looked like, but I dreamed her a thousand different ways. Fiery red hair, blue eyes, freckles from head to toe. Brunette, chestnut eyes, a beauty mark above her lip. Blonde, green eyes, skin like cream, smooth and pale. Black hair, eyes nearly as dark, and chocolate skin. She was always beautiful. And her smell was always the same. Her touch. Her calloused fingertips. Her voice. All the same.

But then Laura started telling me her secrets.

"My name used to be Gretta," she said. "But Laura suits me better, I think. Had to change names after Jim—he was my fiancé—well, I changed it after he killed himself. I couldn't be his Gretta anymore." She stopped scrubbing my back with her sponge and sighed. "I haven't told anyone here about my name. I guess a secret's still a secret if you tell a dead man."

A dead man. The words stung. *Why would she say that? Has something changed?* I imagined a doctor telling my mother I would be gone forever. That I was gone now. *I'm not dead!* I wanted to scream. *Don't let me die!*

I didn't die that day. Or the next. Laura came to see me every few days or so, or at least I think she did. It was hard to tell time as I lay there trapped by my own body. I tried to wake up, to open my eyes, to squeeze my hand, to move a finger. Anything. A panic settled in the pit of my stomach.

They're going to let me die, I thought.

But Laura came again, and I was still alive. This time she didn't talk about my death; she talked about his.

"I felt better after talkin' with you 'bout Jim; I don't wanna talk your ear off…but you don't mind, right? 'Course not," Laura said. "You're a gentleman." She was silent for a few minutes as she took a warm cloth to my face, wiping away sweat and grime. "He was a good man," she whispered. "A soldier. But he lost his leg and wasn't the same when he came back. He hated physical therapy; it made him feel like a failure. I tried to help. Did my best to support him, but I should've listened when he said he wanted to die. I should've helped him go as peacefully as possible," she said with a sniffle. "Then maybe he wouldn't have died like he did. Jumped off a building, but it wasn't tall enough, I guess. He was alive, in agony, for *days* before he died."

I wanted to hold her then, to tell her I was sorry for her loss, but I just laid there, as always, and listened. She finished bathing me without another word, but I could hear her crying.

"I need to talk to someone," she said when she came back again. "I need someone to understand. I don't know if you can hear me…" She paused, and then her breath warmed my ear as she whispered, "I've been workin' to help people like Jim for years. I know what people would say. They'd say I'm a murderer."

My palms begin to sweat.

"They'd say I'm a monster, but I'm not! I'm givin' them a peaceful end! I *am*! Most men just can't handle that kind of loss. The loss of a leg. Jim was a strong man. Stronger than any man I've ever met. And he jumped right off a building."

Oh. Oh no, Laura. What did you do?

"Five men. Five men in the last seven years," she said. "I kept them from windin' up like Jim. Their families remember them as they should be remembered. Strong. Handsome. Whole. Not broken and bloody. Not...not like I saw Jim. Not victims of depression, of suicide."

No, no, no, no, no. I tried to close my ears. I tried not to listen. But I heard every word. *Where's the Laura I love? The one that makes my mother laugh?*

I felt her soft lips kiss my cheek, warm and supple. "I've been keepin' all this locked inside for too long. Feels good to let it out, to tell someone who won't go tellin' the world. A secret's still a secret if you tell a dead man," she said as if a burden had been lifted from her.

That night my dreams of Laura turned to nightmares. I was in the woods, and they smelled like her. I couldn't move. But I could see. There were leaves and mud underneath my limp body, nothing but dark, bare branches rustling in the wind above. And my left leg was gone up to mid-thigh.

A shadow stepped out from behind one of the trees. There was no definition to the creature. No eyes, no hair, no features of any kind. Only a black shadow.

Laura.

As she came closer, her scent was strong enough to make my stomach churn. She was a silhouette, nothing more, but when she knelt beside me and brushed my forehead with her fingers, I could feel the callouses. The shadow pulled out a syringe, black as she was, and plunged the needle into my arm. I tried to scream, but it gargled in my throat and became no more than a moan.

My body is broken. This is what she does to broken men.

I came to in my prison of flesh, and for once, I was thankful to return from my dreams. Things were different after that. Before, I waited for Laura's scent. I pined for her voice. I relished her touch. But after she started telling me her secrets, my heart would race and my palms would sweat whenever she came near.

I have to wake up. I have to. She'll kill me if I don't, I thought when she would come to scrub my body clean.

And then one day I did. All the sudden there was light, blurred and shrouded, but it was there. My fingers twitched, and I was confused. I couldn't remember what happened. Where I was, or why.

"Mr. Barnum?" came a voice. I tensed at the sound of my name; I knew I should be afraid of something, someone, and then I remembered Laura.

That's not Laura's voice. Is she even real? Maybe I've been dreaming.

I blinked over and over, and the room became clearer. I curled my fingers again, and they obeyed. The nurse who said my name was short and thick with a curly knot of blonde hair streaked with grey on top of her head.

"Mr. Barnum? Can you hear me?" she asked. "Blink twice if the answer is yes. Three times if no."

I blinked twice.

"You're at St. Mary's Hospital. You were in an accident. Do you remember?"

I blinked three times. I groaned and I tried to reach the tube that was down my throat, to indicate I wanted it out, but my arm just flopped onto my belly.

"We'll remove the breathing tube; don't worry. And don't try to move too much," the nurse said. "Your muscles are weak."

"Who are you talkin'—" A woman walked into the room, but stopped short at the sight of me. My body tensed as I caught a whiff of her perfume. It was Laura. Her voice. Her scent. She was taller than I thought she'd be. Poker straight brown hair pulled up tight in a ponytail. Freckles dotted her cheeks, and her eyes were a vibrant green. A pretty girl, if I hadn't known better.

"Mr. Barnum is awake," said the short, thick nurse. "I'm going to grab the doctor and get that tube out of his throat so he can start to communicate. Will you stay with him?"

I blinked three times, grunting with each blink. *No, don't leave. Don't leave me with her.* Blink. Blink. Blink.

"'Course I will," said Laura. "I'll look after him 'til you get back." When the nurse was gone, Laura put her hands on her hips. "What am I gonna to do with you?" she said. There was a countertop with drawers underneath, and she opened one. "Your mother was about to pull the plug, you know." She winked at me as she pulled out a little glass bottle. "So here I thought I could tell you things...you might not remember it now—"

Oh, I do.

"—but you might remember soon. Don't worry," she said. "I know how to make your passin' peaceful." She filled a syringe with the liquid in the glass bottle.

I began to squirm, to grunt. I banged my head on the bed, but it made only a muffled thump against the soft pillow. She came closer, stopping beside the IV drip. She smiled as she injected the liquid into the IV.

And as a burning sensation went up my arm, as my heart began to beat so fast and hard that it hurt, as my body began to tremble, Laura leaned close, held my hand, and whispered, "Sorry, honey. A secret's only a secret if you tell it to a dead man."

To Be Cold
by Karen Mocker Dabson

As Jo stood on the beach, the wind worried the black fur trim of her parka. It brushed her cheeks and detoured down the front of her neck before she could rearrange her scarf. She seized the muffler's long wooly arms, but dropped them again to let the cold breeze have its way with her. She inhaled deeply, tasting the shards of clean mountain air in the back of her throat.

Snow had smothered what little there was of the shoreline. As though a vast vat of icing had spilled, the white blanket spread along the water's edge undulating around and over rocks and disguising last night's grizzly bear visit.

Jo had traveled to this deserted beach to escape the sweltering conditions of late May at home. There, Mother Nature had cranked up the dial on the thermostat, and John had been turning every conversation into a forest fire. When that happened, she sank within herself and contemplated coolness in all its forms – snow, ice, freshwater springs, Norwegian fjords, polar ice caps, frozen tundra – on and on until she could shut the hot away. One day, she realized that she would melt if she did not find, physically find, the cold.

This morning, she stood on the snow-shrouded strand of Lake Louise, breathing the minty freshness of new snow and listening to the blessed silence. In its desolate beauty, the lake had lured her from the prescribed footpath and onto its shores. Ice, like the finest Venetian glass, swirled away in obscure patterns and covered the entire face of the lake. Its opaque surface shone jewel-like, a vivid aquamarine beaming with an intensity and depth that epitomized the cold she sought.

On the beach, the ice climbed into a third dimension. Shards rose in tall, Chihuly-style sculptures. Columns of chilled, clear glass splayed one against another as they reached for the sky. Each time the lake froze, thawed, and froze again, the structures shifted and struck new poses. The blues and purples and peaches of the sunrise dwelt within them, and the spectacle of iced lake and ice fantasia captured and held Jo in its thrall.

Her fleecy mukluks carved a bluish scar through the snow as she walked from the beach to the edge of the lake. Now Jo stepped onto the ice, no longer resisting its call. Her boots skated easily over the smooth surface. Ahead, Jo saw a glow and schussed towards it. Shortly, she stopped in the midst of a luminescence that swathed her in ribbons of aqua and white. Her head pounded like an adrenaline rush, and biting her cheek, she tasted blood and salt. Her eyes ached as she gazed down into the lake. She had only ever read of such illumination in books but here it dwelt, paradise locked below the ice.

At first, Jo's breath came in short, excited puffs. All the while, tendrils of chill wound by the fur of her boots, curled up the sleeves of the green parka, and vined down her back, passing through the layers – first the down, then the wool, past the silk to the skin, the dear flesh where it longed to be as much as Jo longed for it. The cold wrapped her as deftly as the snow had draped the beach.

"Oh." Jo sighed from the bottom of her lungs. In a distant way, she became aware of the growing susurrus that drifted from the tops of the tall pines lining the lake – the only acknowledgment of her being in this vast desert of snow, snow bank, and ice sculpture.

Jo knelt on all fours to embrace the light. A new pattern crackled out within the ice beneath her. She kissed the hard cold. It kissed her in return, tasting of stones and minerals, mountains and streams. Her gloved hands glided before her until her thighs, her stomach, her bosom, her cheek rested on the frosty coolness.

High above, a juvenile eagle keened, his mournful echo filling the sky; and then, she slept.

Unlocking the Past
by Debra Sutton

Sometimes I wish I could get out of my own head. My own skin. Maybe, be someone else for a while. But it's just a fleeting thought. I'm proud of who I am. What I've accomplished. But the anger's in here, bruising my soul as it thrashes around trying to escape. It's had years to build up, poisoning every word, every deed. I work so hard to forget the past, I really do. But how can I when I'm reminded of it every day? People watching me, pretending nothing's wrong. They are silently judging me. Blaming me for something I can't control. Just get over it they say. As if those words are easy. I can tell you, they're not. Because I've tried. I feel like I'm always trying. They sent me here because they said you could help. But that's not true, is it? You can't understand.

I jab the button, stopping the tape, but I can't stop the words replaying in my head. She's right. How can I understand? I can't see the pain that permeates every aspect of her life. I know it's there just out of sight, and if I shift my focus fast enough, maybe I can catch a glimpse. But I never can. I want to understand. It's more than just my job. Someone her age should be reaching out to the possibilities of the world, building a new life full of hope and idealism. And it might be crushed later by reality. But not now. Not so soon. Not before her life really begins. They forced her to come see me. An incident, they'd said. She wears her resistance like a shield; her arms crossed, her body rigid. Scars weave through her skin like a tapestry, some jagged edges visible, some not.

I'm amazed by the honesty in her voice-on her face. How can I help her heal the deep wounds she carries? Overcome the fear that's bright in her world and barely noticeable in mine? If you believe the papers on my wall, I'm a counselor. Someone who helps. Sometimes I don't believe the papers. Sometimes I can't help.

I can't understand. Maybe it's because I've never experienced even a portion of the pain she lives with every day. Maybe it's because I've never had to walk on eggshells wondering from where the next danger will come.

Maybe it's because I've seen too much, and I should take those damn papers off my wall.

And maybe, just maybe, it's because I'm white.

Wild Love

by Rexanna Ipock-Brown

Cyrus opened his eyes. The humid summer air layered with the fresh green scent of grass, fertile soil, and car exhaust tickled his nose. Safe for the moment, he relaxed. Grateful for the quiet valley tucked into a patch of woods, Cyrus had slept undisturbed for the first time in days. New at being on his own, he frowned, contemplating his next move. An insistent belly rumble decided for him. Time to eat. He stood, stretched, and moving like water flowed from the woods.

A whiff of bacon drew him through suburban streets. His feet ambled along the rough concrete enjoying the cool feel on his skin. The aroma of roses painted in the colors of the sunset snagged his attention. A peek in the backyard beyond the rose bush resulted in the possibility of food for later. He believed in being prepared.

At the beginning of summer, Cyrus thought he was prepared. Not so. Nothing had equipped him for the noisy machines tearing up the earth and his family's home. Dreams of snuggling with his mate in their soft bed, warm and secure, haunted him. A gaze at possible home sites reminded him of the need to find her. With a shake of his fur coat, Cyrus let the hate of not knowing settle.

He continued to make his way through the familiar neighborhood, giving a wide berth to a particular house. Not wide enough though. The twang of old copper assaulted his senses. His empty stomach growled in revulsion. In a loud voice a man bragged while blood and the stench of death rolled off a pickup. No matter how much cologne the man poured on himself, the stink prevailed. Cyrus recognized a bully when he smelled one. A shudder passed through his body.

A deep fear drove through his chest. What if this man had trapped his mate or worse? He bared his teeth, imagining what he'd like to do to him. Cyrus slipped behind the shrubs and maneuvered closer. Ethel, his mate was not among the dead. A great anger tinged with sadness shot through him as he caught sight of coyotes' lifeless bodies piled in the truck bed. He lowered his head in reverence. The knowledge he couldn't bring them back reminded him to choose his battles. With a burst of speed, Cyrus cut through another yard to connect to the sidewalk leading to the source of the bacon.

One sniff led him to a large building where humans congregated in the morning. A collection of people with backpacks and sleeping bags stood in a line leading into the front door. With cautious steps he made his way to the back entrance where a plate of eggs and bacon waited for him. A woman's face appeared between the curtains of a window, watching for him. She never tried to come near him although he suspected she wouldn't harm him. That was okay with him. *Always mistrust humans.* That rule kept him alive.

With one eye on the lookout, he licked the plate clean in seconds. Raising his head, his gaze connected with the woman's. Her lips lifted into a grin, and she gave him a nod of her head. He tipped his nose in a salute to her kindness before slipping into the wooded area with a silent and swift stride.

With hunger no longer riding him, his thoughts turned to finding his wild love. Deep in his heart he sensed she still lived. He craved her spirit and her touch. She inspired him to live. Ethel mistrusted all humans, going berserk when spotting them. His lips quirked up at the corners remembering her running for their den if one came too close.

Surely, she'd found a haven. Ethel's instincts often lead them to secluded spots. They had been hiding in their home concealed by a wooded patch until the bulldozers ripped it apart. She ran, squealing across a busy street, while he took the opposite direction. That night he returned sniffing every bush and tree in hopes she lived. With a deep breath, he had allowed relief to visit for the moment. No dead bodies.

Several days passed, and now, fear dogged his every step. Where was she? Cyrus trotted along the sidewalk leading back into the neighborhood he visited this morning. A familiar odor wafted his way. Head up and back, he drew in air reading the news it brought. The spoor stopped him in his tracks for a moment. The bushes covered him as he slunk into the bully's front yard. A large metal cage sat square in the middle of the lawn. A primal anger flooded Cyrus. Trapped inside, his mate paced back and forth. The pickup and the pack of men were gone. Collecting his courage, he flew to her side.

Her pleading whine revealed Ethel's terror. One look told him she was unharmed. Panic rose in him as he pawed the lock on the door to no avail. Cyrus licked her face through the wire, showing his love. He stopped, scenting a human in the area. His eyes sought out the person, preparing to fight for his mate's life. Hope rose in him at the sight of the woman who gave him meat, walking down the sidewalk. Cyrus nuzzled Ethel to reassure her, then strolled towards the woman.

She paused, watching him. Panic flashed in her scent as she stood still. He lowered his head and tucked his tail hoping she would understand.

"Hey, you're my breakfast buddy, aren't you?" Her eyes tracked him. Step by step he slowly turned and worked his way back to the front yard and the cage. Comprehension dawned on her face. With careful paces, she followed him.

With a soft yip to calm his mate, the coyote raised his eyes to the woman and let out a low woof. His amber eyes pleaded with her, trying to communicate.

With slow movements she came closer to the trap. Frightened yelps broadcasted Ethel's alarm. The human became a statue of stone. With a yip and growl Cyrus finally calmed her.

The woman whispered, "It's okay. I'm here to help you." Her gentle voice flowed over the coyotes reducing their anxiety. She reached for the cage door and cautiously touched the lock. A low growl from Ethel made her pause, but when both coyotes stayed still, she fitted the key hanging on the cage door into the lock.

The door swung open permitting the female coyote to race for freedom. The woman stepped back, allowing Cyrus to catch up with Ethel halfway across the yard. She took a cue from him and paused.

With a glance back, Cyrus studied the woman as she smashed the lock on the door and tossed the key into the overgrown evergreen in the neighbor's yard. She nodded her head in their direction. "See you two for breakfast." She said, heading to the sidewalk.

Overjoyed to find his mate, Cyrus nipped, rubbed, and nuzzled her. She led him to a valley punctuated by a creek. He followed her into a den twice the size of their old one and marveled at the luxurious grasses and leaves lining the grotto. Cyrus curled around her, and they slept.

After a couple of days, Cyrus and Ethel ventured out to the large building with food. Two plates sat on the ground by the back door. They padded with soft steps to the food and ate. Finished, they gave a nose salute to the woman in the window and headed home.

On the way, they passed the street where the bully lived. The commotion caused by the cars with bright flashing lights on top caught their curiosity. They watched from the bushes as the man struggled to walk through his front door.

Hands bound by metal, his face puckered into a storm cloud. Two humans tucked him into one of the waiting cars and closed the door. Cyrus and his love grinned as they crept close to stare at him through the opposite window of the car.

He stunk of old blood and rotten flesh mingled with cheap cologne. Even the coyotes found the odor unpleasant. Cyrus sneezed, alerting him to their presence. Eyes narrowed to slits, the man yelled for the others. Cyrus and Ethel vanished into the landscaping, but not before they heard the humans laughing at the bully for imagining things.

Photo by Nancy Jo Cegla

A Brief Encounter
by Terry Allen

First Place

Image you are asked
to describe Ebenezer Scrooge
by a space alien from one
of the 17 billion earth-sized
planets in our galaxy for some reason
that seems very important to him.
Naturally, you want to be helpful
because you remember the time
you got lost in Cleveland

and so how do you respond
to the alien? How do you get to the heart
of the matter? Do you say
if anyone knows how to keep
Christmas well, it's Ebenezer Scrooge,
and then quickly add that you'll
explain Christmas later. Do you
say that Scrooge was as good
a man as this world ever knew,

and that if people laughed at his high
spirits, generosity and good cheer
that he was wise enough to know
that nothing ever happens in this world
for good at which some people do not
have their fill of laughter

or do you answer the alien's
question by reaching into a worn
bag of tired bits and pieces and pull out
a handful of words like *tight-fisted, cold,
covetous old sinner*,

and if you do, might you not
be surprised that the visitor
shakes his head and turns away

and somehow you know
in that moment
that he'll return home and report
that he visited a world
where it's inhabitants
don't yet understand
or believe
in redemption.

Night, Mid-February
by Terry Allen

rain and sleet turn to snow
the road disappears—

bright haloed lights ahead
approaching too fast,

sky and earth become one
in the wintery darkness

are you in the right lane
you wonder
as you hold tight to the wheel

and drive ever forward
toward home

Horror
by Peg Crawford

Blood red seeping through the cloth in scarlet
streaks on sinless white. No sound, no movement,
no one knew the gory battle fought and
won…They lay in crimson puddles through the
night.
    I found the wounded in the morning
light, and started searching for the next of kin.
Regret cannot reverse what reckless brings,
I'll never wash the reds with whites again!

Mr. Snapper Flapper
by Larry Allen

Bright orange
He stands in the parking lot
Vigorously
Snapping and waving
Saluting and pointing
Trying so hard to grab attention
Traffic accidents result

But imagine you were he
First, he is plastic
And he stands all day and all night
Snapping and waving and saluting and pointing
With strong gusts of hot air blowing up his butt

Really, it's not much of a job
But somebody has to do it

I wonder if the man who set him up
Is still on site
He should be worried
That any moment
Mr. Snapper Man might break loose
And, with a violent series
Of snaps and salutes
Fly across that parking lot
And go right for the throat.

A Box of Old Pictures
by James Coffman

The large plastic box
Slides out of storage; the dust,
Having died trying to penetrate
Its secrets, is wiped away.
The contents are spread
Before us, those photos—
Glossy, matt, sepia—all
Out of order, history's attempt
At shuffling itself.

Faces—unblinking, some forgotten—
Look at us, accusing us,
And we are surprised who came
To the opening. The fault clearly
Lies with whomever forgot
To disinvite some of the players.
This box of old pictures has not
Kept up, is truly out of sync.

We'll put the box away,
But not before we remove the takes
So terribly out of focus,
And with our scissors we'll alter
Some group shots, purging us
Of memories always wrong.
We know what our history is—
Or should be—now the box
Of old pictures knows it too.

A Fly
by James Coffman

A fly went buzzing
Across my dash,
Wedging herself between
The windshield and A/C vent.

She resisted every attempt
Of mine to shoo her
Out the window, unsmiling,
Looking for a spot to lay her eggs.

She was to me a minor irritant
With all my many jobs to do,
Yet she, driven to drop her eggs,
Had only a day to do it.

A Visit to Grandma's House
by Eva Ridenour

Mom called it "The Aunt Lucy Burton Place."
A half-mile from the main road on
a one-lane path that ended
at a white two-story house.
Grandma had sold her farm north of town
as she feared Grandpa might kill the neighbor,
with whom he had a long-running quarrel,
and they moved south of town.

I remember being there only once.

A town girl used to a one-storied house,
I became fascinated with the stairs,
tried to climb them, but Mom called me back.
Dust particles danced in the sunrays on the top landing,
I imagined a great treasure up there,
but to my disappointment
found a room with only one metal bed.

My two bachelor uncles slept in the living room.
Grandpa's brother,
who in pictures looked a lot like him,
white hair, blue bibbed overalls, gaunt,
until a couple of years before,
had occupied the other upstairs bedroom.

We got up at 5 a.m.,
ate the breakfast Grandma had started cooking at 4 a.m.
Meal over and men off to feed animals,
I escaped to play beneath a grape arbor
which offered a canopy of comfort

from my strange surroundings.

Sometimes, all these years later,
I catch the pungent odor of
sultry summer sunlight evaporating
the dew from a nearby catalpa tree.

All Day the Media
by James Coffman

Have promised snow,
Their prophets as confident
As the Michelin Man.

The sky is darkly gray
While random leaves blow
Curlicues and loop-the-loops,
Then bed themselves to ground.

First flakes come
Like airy ashes
From a campfire, cold,
Now blown upon.

Ice crystals never touch;
The building blocks do not connect,
But swirl, endlessly,
Until they die away.

The children wait, eyes upward,
Arms outstretched like cornhusk dolls.
Small puffs ascend like smoke signals
From their red and running noses.

Darkness, like a stocking cap, pulls itself
Over the eyes of the watchers,
And the children slog inside,
Sleds and shovels standing guard.

Alone on Stage
by Billie Holladay Skelley

In scene one, I gave you my heart.
In scene two, you laughed and tore it apart.
Now I'm starring in "Love Gone Astray,"
And it's a part I never ever wanted to play.

Other actors bellow, "You'll love again."
But they don't understand the pain that I'm in.
I'm trapped in the spotlights between Heaven and Hell,
But even blinded I see there are no more tickets to sell.

Never again will my fate be put on the marquee,
So some unknown director can annihilate me.
Better to perform alone on life's revolving stage,
Than find motivation purely in agony and rage.

No, I'll never again star on this stage of regret,
Waiting for the script to reveal some new threat.
I'll lock my heart in a cage and chain it to the floor,
Just so I never ever have to play this role anymore.

Black Cat
by Sheree Nielsen

Black cat ponders
outside wonders –
crisp leaves whistling down
brisk autumn wind.

Mellifluous
Carolina chickadees
dance the jig
on wood rails,
foraging for seeds,
left by humans.

Black cat
rests comfortably
on the buttercream
cotton rug,
sun glistening,
warming coal black fur.

Black cat ponders life,
outside the big glass door,
tail swaying
to and fro
lemon eyes observing….
she secures a spot
near Red Dog.

The two
touch paw to paw
reposed
in the noonday sun.

Campfire
by Kayla Nilges

Fire dancing;
hearken back to better days

Languishing the secret even still
Long after the secret is no longer

Because you live in present day,
and as seasons persist,
I do not.

In the mausoleum
In the tomb

The stars barely noticed when you took your leave.

Catalpas
by Eva Ridenour

When catalpas bloom in Missouri
rain and mother nature have painted
the land shades of emerald, forest and pine.

Clusters of alabaster blossoms
make beautiful bridal bouquets
among large dense leaves.

I wonder what use the beans can be.
They hang to limbs
long after leaves fall away,

pencil thin, crooked, ugly, useless.
But they must have a purpose,
if only to make more trees.

I am reminded of the winter
when I chanced to burn the remains
of one in the fireplace.

How I enjoyed watching the flames
blue, white, yellow and orange
consume the wood while

making my room cozy and warm.

Cave Man
by Lee Ann Russell

A man must walk in forests green
and stumble on the path
to hunt for food and slay the bull
and face his neighbor's wrath.

But, every season, without fail,
a pounding knock is heard,
and once again, he journeys forth
to fortify and gird.

So, often man must go alone
into his quiet cave
as solace for the loneliness
that worldliness engraved.

He knows exactly where the cave
will lie upon his map;
a fantasy or rocky ledge
will answer to his tap.

"I'll be back soon," he softly calls
unto his loving mate,
"And when I am, we both shall know
'twas worth the measured wait."

The cave stands empty, firm and proud,
the stanchion of the gate
within which man will be enshrined
and answer to his fate.

He enters stooped, but stretches tall
to gauge his amplitude.
He reaches forth to touch the walls
and feel again, renewed.

A haven waits within the cave,
and echoes loudly call,
resounding with their master's voice,
reflecting rise and fall.

The cavern cool, yet comfortable,
embraces as he sits,
to build a fire to warm his soul
and lovingly acquit.

Withdraw, he must, for time alone
to think and fuss and swear,
to sit upon the throne of "Man,"
and live in solitaire.

No visitors are 'ere allowed;
no one to interrupt.
There's room for only one inside,
and only one to sup.

A dragon guards the opening
and breathes a fire of rust
inflaming those who'd come within
who violate his trust.

When time has passed within the cave,
and moisture fills his face,
stalagmites grow wherein he stood
and strengthen with his grace.

A solid rock enshrines the cave
and beautifies its host,
and stands as sentry to the core
as life is diagnosed.

He slides along the muddy floor,
and slips and slides again,
then gains his footing carefully
as sunlight trickles in.

A consciousness of dampness reigns,
and cold and wet and chill,
as sun becomes a glistening veil
awakening his will.

Celestial orb expands his view,
illuminating worth,
surrounding dark within his realm,
permitting man's rebirth.

The cave grows smaller, dim and tight;
it squeezes every vein.
While rescuing his very soul,
it binds his every aim.

So, quickly does he douse the fire,
and pick up all debris,
and once again, he journeys forth,
and once again, he's free.

Chains
by C.A. Simonson

Shackled by chains, I was bound by sin
My mind tormented and torn within.
Harassed by greed: beat a silent doom
Chained to my past in a self-made tomb.

The links were chains in my fettered mind,
Peace, joy, and love– unable to find.
Chains confined me from entrance to peace
Imprisoned and jailed with no release.

Religions, cults, philosophies tried;
Just cold, dark cells in which to hide.
Men and free drugs wreaked havoc on life
Headed downhill with endless strife.

Then a man said, "I will love you."
So I believed, and went with him too.
Confused, troubled, frustrated, alone.
I yearned for freedom, but none was found.

Then another man spoke straight to me,
"I have a plan to set you free."
"Would he hurt me? Abuse me again?
Leave me strangling alone in sin?

He told of his love and how he had died,
Offered me hope with new life supplied.
Yearned to believe; his words, were they true?
Could I trust him? Would he hurt me too?

But I took the chance and left my past.
His words were true! I'm free at last!
True love, peace, and joy from above
Given by Jesus: the Man I love.

Choroidal Nevus
by Nancy Jo Cegla

The optometrist's lips purse
the collection of consonants
and vowels that form like a kiss
about to be bestowed with love,
but—like love—an arrow
is set free with force piercing
my heart. Her words
come from under water bubbling
up slowly like a clutch of balloons
from a child's hand,
but popping like my spirit
deflating one molecule
after another.
Pop! Pop! Pop!

She asks the obligatory question:
Have you suffered trauma to your eyes?
I want to answer:
No more than the average baby boomer.
The question rings like a clapper
striking the interior metal of a cast bell,
and I want to say:
No more than the average abused wife.
She tries again to resuscitate my attention
with the question:
Have your eyes suffered any trauma?
And I see

an assassinated president's
young son salute the passing casket
draped with red, white, and blue
stars and stripes, and that president's
brother lying in a pool of blood
slowly draining from his head
surrounded by helpless hands.
I see the soul of a Black nation grieved by a bullet
and yet another added to the alphabet soup
of the 1960s. I see men walk on the moon
while tiny, black, bloated bellies
want for food at home and abroad.
I see race riots, anti-war protests, a lying president,
hostages in foreign lands. Money
pouring into pockets to elect a puppet president
of a party determined to crown him with laurels
for decades to come. I see the roots
of future wars send out tendrils
deep below the soil that will surface
like blades of grass to be mowed down
across vast oceans. I see mothers abused
by fathers, brothers assault sisters,
police shoot the unarmed. I see dynamite
strapped to young, pregnant women
who hold the hands of children
as they march together toward armored
vehicles exploding many parts
from the once whole. I see decapitated
tourists, reporters, and aid workers.
I see stars in my right eye one dark night
as his fist strikes me blackening the socket
for one week. I see the church
to which I have lived faithfully give ear
to black words on white paper
crafted by a lying cheat to defame me.
I see hope of marriage to the man I love
slip from my fingers when I hear the diagnosis
"choroidal nevus," and the words that follow:
I'm sending you to a cancer specialist.

And she asks once more,
Have your eyes suffered any trauma?
I answer, *"No."*

Circumvent
by Kayla Nilges

I walked to the chair in the dark,
and your spectre followed me there,
marking the map on my heart,
letting the memory lie bare,
saving your place in the night,
holding out hope it is real
But nothing is right,
nothing is right,
until flesh and bone is here.

The Corner Café
by Nancy Jo Cegla

I unroll the paper napkin, reflexively rubbing the spoon's bowl.
Each weekend, we two have breakfast at the Corner Café—
something of a slice of Americana.
As I thumb the menu,
I see the usual and consider history.
I order the French toast which tastes of almonds.
It's not that I don't select other dishes,
but I have my favorites, like waitresses do.
The owner's name is "Eboni,"
and her hair curls like glossy, black crayon shavings
and rests upon plump shoulders.
All who enter are greeted with "Good morning!", and a pearly smile.
She wears black.
She brings coffee to my lover.
She asks what I want today as I'm less predictable. I order hot chocolate
even though it is July, but the air is cool, for it is still early.
Earlier than usual, really, for I plan to drive to Wisconsin this morning,
and I wish to beat the traffic. I'm concerned about my sister's
odd behavior. Nothing new, really, just more.
The hot chocolate arrives, it is predictably powdery
and mounded in whipped cream.
I spoon the mountain of white, savoring its sweetness on my tongue:
cool and melting.
My lover pours a creamer, stirs, the dark coffee dissolves caramel colored,
like our waitress's complexion. Her voice is also creamy, but with Egyptian accent

like ancient flute rifts inspired by Hathor's inventive, loving music.

My eyes take in the room, but—because it is early—I see no one I know.
A tall man is folded into a booth.
My eyes focus on the wall above him in a ceiling corner
where a spray of roses cling: a centuries old, powerful symbol.
To Egyptians, the rose is more than love and beauty;
more than healing, or even aphrodisiac: it connects life to afterlife.
The man is a police officer, and his friend sits in a wheelchair
looking accustomed to it. The man unfolds his body
and rises to find tabasco sauce for his iron-sided friend.
Former partners in the force?
I imagine a hail of bullets and the partner taking one
in the spine for the other in an act of brotherly love.
The bond between partners in the force, is a love
known by men on the battlefield: this looks like survivor's guilt.
Guilt is what I think is fueling my sister's behavior,
for she has driven a wedge into my life in my daughter's estrangement.
I doubt she expected to have taken so much from me.
For her it was a game, and games offer amusement.
Ancient Romans enjoyed casting Christians to the lions
as a form of entertainment—but at a cost.

She grows older and looks unhealthy—as guilt will do—
like overripe fruit neither young, nor mature, but simply decaying.
Yet I love her and find myself driving one-hundred miles
to talk with her, and shed some light.

Love is strange. I turn my eyes back to the roses.
I recall that Egyptian roses flourish in sun,
are reborn in spring, and have magical healing powers
through the love goddess, Isis.

I reach across the sticky table,
our fingers entwine,
and our hands are warm.

The Crows
by Peg Crawford

"I wonder what they want" she said, "The crows,
just staring, standing there, beneath that tree
just waiting. Look." she turned and watched him rip
another paper from the book, then crumple,
toss it on the flame, then rip in quick
succession more,
> *Crumple, crumple, toss and*
> *burn and cast the paper in the fire, then*
> *stir it with a walking stick to spread the*
> *glowing ashes well in ritualistic*
> *burning of the evidence on pyre.*

"They know," she turned away and tapped the glass
to try to spook the birds, "They know…"
"They don't,"
he said, "they're only birds. Now come and help
me with this rug, and mind the little shards
of vase. We need to clean up quickly now,
and then we need to pack and leave this place."

The Crows remained for half a day, ensuring
that the bones were clean, and every leaf was
picked and turned and everything was as it
was before…and then they flew away.

Dark Lullaby
by Laura Seabaugh

Sleep, love, forever sleep
Dream for me the sweetest dream
Dream your secrets dark and deep
Secrets only you can keep

Dream, love, and as you do
I will also dream of you
May your nightmares be few
And may all your dreams come true

Elfin Heart
by James Coffman

They point us
To the waiting room,
Drenched with the stench
Of early morning coffee,

And strewn with magazines
—torn and bent—
From another year.
    —No news to share.

We wait
While seconds pound
Like slams
Of an iron hammer.

Daydreams are nightmares
And scalpels, scythes.
And not knowing
Is the cruelest pain of all.

Your heart, my child,
Is the size of your fist,
So miniscule,
So hard to see.

Your baby heart,
So hard to work around
Even for the best
Of pulmonary surgeons.

In our best of fantasies
We see your little body
With its elfin heart—
Limp, compliant.

We can do no less
This day but follow your lead
And hush our fears,
    Be still.
    Be still.

Evidence of a Still Life
by Peg Crawford

She turned the fruit, a Fuji blushed with amber,
to the right. Then paused, withdrew and squinted
stereoscopic blurring sight to try
to see the story told in camera view.
The brilliance of the apple stunned the lesser
lemon's fame, so out it came to find its
home below and left in yielding deference,
snug against the puddled velvet, casual
in careful drape around the bowl to
cradle grapes, then spill a waterfall of
red beyond the table out of frame.
If only she had saved the little raven
corpse she rescued from the cat, still warm, but
quickly pushed the morbid thought away and
opted for an empty cage whose open
door would hint of something sans the truth…
The occupant had simply died with age.
He paused a moment at the door to watch
her turn, then turn again each player on
the farmhouse table stage, then left without
goodbye, his shadow just a spectral
interruption in a footnote on a page.
She brushed the filmy curtains to the side.
7:05 the sun would rise and start
the play with cool white light that mellowed then
to softer yellow. A bright crisp light that
only lived between the dark and fully day.
She set her camera, shutter speed and angle,
height to capture what she saw, to say what
words could never say…
then checked her watch and

sat with hands in lap and face to dawn, to wait.

Free Pain Evaluation for You or Your Horse

*(Sign painted on a trailer
in Columbia, Missouri)*

by Terry Allen

Have you ever had your horse travel
freely in a circle to the right,
but fight you tooth and nail
when you ask for the other direction?

Have you been running around
in circles, but only to the right
to avoid the fires of hell and holy damnation
when you might go the other direction?

Does your horse have a contracted heel
on one foot that won't get any better
despite the best efforts
of your hoof care professional?

Have you or your horse been battling
performance or lameness issues
and don't know what to do next
except to flare your nostrils, hang your head
and walk slowly to the right?

I'll be down the road from your place,
Thursday next
and can stop by to take a look see.

I can't perform miracles,
but I'll do the best I can
for the horse.

Headstone Hopping
by James Coffman

No teacher in Newman or Hume
Nor Indianapolis was like Mrs. Brown
In the country school who knew
How important was a cemetery to recess.

It was an enchanted playground
Of evergreen trees and headstones,
Of limestone, granite and marble,
My Field of Dreams, my Oz.

Standing or flat,
The tombstones were perfect,
Inventive fun, building blocks
For cities, tunnels, recesses.

The stones were our bases,
Our hurdles, our hidey holes,
Our lily pads—no questions
Of ethics or propriety.

Could *we* ask more
At *our* time of rest
Than for children, unafraid,
Leaping and laughing above us?

Here There Be Dragons
by Peg Crawford

No glorious battlefield death scene speech,
no final words of truth to keep or carry
like a guarding shield against the wounds that
never heal…No clap of thunder, banging
shutters sudden with mysterious breath.
No harps or trumpets or blinding light, not
even a flutter, or whispered regrets
of things I remembered and things you'd forget.
It all fell to mist like the words to a
tune, then shrank to a world that could fit in
a room with you on a raft and I on
the shore, the ceiling for sky and a void
past the door…I struggle to reach you
to stand by your side and keep you from drifting
away with the tide…
but here there be dragons
I cannot fight.
I cannot win.
I cannot right this wrong, but only hold your
hand and stay until the journey takes you home…
Cause here there be dragons you'll battle alone.

In The Garden
by Maril Crabtree

Nestled among stones, clusters of spider webs shine
in the sun, spun across spored fronds of low-growing fern,
woven at crazy-quilt angles, tilting up
at the sky like miniature hammocks, each with a tiny spider
the size of a child's fingernail.
Some webs show ragged holes. Each time the wind blows
it seems they might tear off their moorings, floating away
into daylight's bright air.

What makes stones solid and webs so fragile?
Where do we humans fit in
with our clusters and colonies spun so blithely
across the earth's crust, tilting at still-blue skies
ragged with ozone holes,
basking in bright ribbons of emissions crisscrossing the planet?
We sigh, drink tea, listen to the wind, and wonder
with each passing gust whose house will fall next.

Key Exchange
by Danyele Read

Days will come, then go
While you're running, running to and fro

One day you'll be older, but will you be wiser?
One day you'll be older, and what will you see?

Being and doing
Seasons renewing

One day you'll be older, but will you be wiser?
One day you'll be older, and who will you be?

Exchange time for treasure
On the road you are traveling

One day you'll be older, but will you be wiser?
One day you'll be older, and will you be free?

For wisdom brings rubies, that's only the start
Wisdom's not knowledge, she's the pulse of the heart

One day you'll be older, but will you be wiser?
One day you'll be older, but will you hold the key?

Kill Your Darlings
by Peg Crawford

For every open book exists a dozen
chapters mangled red with ink, and scratched and
lined and tossed, then rescued, searched for any
jewels to dazzle, maybe blind the sight of
those who try to read between the lines.
Feed the gossips little bits to drink and
spill as carelessly as water on bricks,
then pull your knife and kill the ones you saved,
the darlings, slash their throats and bury them
without regret, and take it to your grave.

The Last Crossing
by Terry Allen

our poor ship cuts a path
across the smooth surface
of the great lake's
bluish black water

sailing on through the night
beyond the point of no return
before autumn gales blow

before November conjures
ferocious storms
with waves that eat ships whole

a hushed voice tells
of the blinding blizzard
and violent winds
of the White Hurricane
that pulled a dozen good ships
down into an icy tomb

and the surface undulates
and we begin to roll
as if a giant beast
breathing hard
awakens from a long sleep

the biting scent of dank
decayed timber
rises and fog creeps
in from the horizon
as the ghostly moon

blinks in and out of focus

on the edge of expectant winds
distant cannon fire rolls
across the water
with faint cracked voices
chanting a repetitive song

…to thee all angels…
to thee the heavens…

we strain to listen
and peer into the darkness
as a splintered apparition
emerges from the haze

a sailing ship
covered in ice
its sails in ribbons
torn to shreds

bearing down upon us
closing quickly
as if pushed
by a great hand

nearer it comes,
pulling the shrouded fog with it
the unmistakable figure head
illuminated for a moment
by the ringed moon

an eagle's head
with wings and lion's body
plunges through the surging waves

her lights close upon us
revealing seven small cannon

…but not a living soul on board

our captain sounds the alarm
and men shout above the storm
in fear that we will collide
but our ship passes through her

…and the phantom dissipates

blown apart by great gales
sixty tons of sailing ship
built by French explorers
having never returned
from her maiden voyage
before America was America

forever lost
the ghost ship
sails on and on
into the night,
riding the storm

it sails on
into the fog
of time
it sails on…

with us
we know
not far behind

The Last Purr
by Susan Koenig

First came the Harley,
then the 50th Anniversary Mustang,
then the accident.
The Harley was fine, his clutch leg was not.

First I chauffeured while the Mustang sat under lock and key,
then I drove the Mustang when he took my hybrid sedan,
then I drove the Mustang every day.
Me driving the Mustang.
Purrrrrrrrrrrrr

First came crutches and a boot and a cane,
then the driving range, then nine holes, then eighteen,
then unannounced one day,
he's driving the Mustang.
Grrrrrrrrrrrrr

First I demanded joint custody,
then I proposed trading cars for his safety,
then I relented for possession on Saturdays. Now,
we're driving the Mustang.
Purrrrrrrrrrrrr

The Light
by C.A. Simonson

Despondent
Confined. Helpless.
Struggling, pressing, straining.
Depressed, exhausted. Light? Hope!
Determining, building, strengthening
Anticipation. Freedom.
Exhilaration!

Measures to Destiny
by Jessica Faulkner

Blocks of time given to all who have
ever lived on this earth.
Be they brief or spanning decades.
The breadth of time translating into
lines of experiences and spaces of
questionable pasts and futures
of . . . the unknown.
Whether there be more spaces than
lines, they all lend to the quality and fate
of our sole existence.
And when destiny does dictate the final
measure of our lone song,
be there only hopes that a lifetime of
prose and actions might influence the
choices of others, allowing our spirits
to take comfort knowing that we lent,
even a minute spark of meaning,
contribution and influence on this world.
And that the spaces might have meaning
too as crucial pauses taken to ponder the
next steps to our fate.
And *these* moments, are best locked away
as the thoughts and feelings, known only
by . . . One.

The Mole Man
by Larry Allen

Like something from a 50s horror
movie, he appears at my door.
Clawing into his shirt pocket
he produces a small square of paper.

Seventy Five dollars per mole!
Don't I even get to see the corpse?
How do I know it's mine?

His muzzle twitches a bit
and he squints
as he shambles off.
Later I see him setting
up more of his little flags.
Mining my yard
for little brown nuggets of gold.

Night Train
by Eva Ridenour

Late at night,
the freight train whistle whines
off in the distance.
As the engine and
its load lumber toward town.
The pitch is higher
when the signal sounds at
the crossing in town.

My dog howls, mournful and long,
apparently, the sound hurts his ears.

The train moves on, and on,
for what seems like an hour,
but is probably ten minutes until
silence again claims the night.

What toxic substance
has just passed through our town?
I sigh, turn over and go back to sleep.
We've again avoided
the headlines on the morning news.

The Oak-Branch Cross
by Pablo Baum

She felt no sorrow, no bitter hate,
for she could not know the splendor
of the world that lay beyond the chains,
chains she'd not yet seen nor felt,
contempt she'd not yet sensed.
No loathsome fiend yet battered her
to leave his seed to burden her
without the love that gives to one
a meaning for this life.

Mother strove with brother sister,
all consumed by toil and sun and sweat and dust
to gladden folks atop the hill,
folks who dined and played and drank strange swills
that made them sway then laugh then fall.
She knew not yet that there was beauty,
there were brooks to splash and play,
and there were meadows vibrant, verdant
made as much for her,
for mother brother sister, neighbor
there to savor touch and dream.

Our giggling blossom prattled on
as Grim One thwarted all from
pleasures simple, pleasures lovely,
nothing more than dangling toes in babbling brooks,
or watching clouds drift lazily by,
or making plans to live and love
—all forbidden lest they shrink the harvest.

Grim One pounced at orange rays,

hosting lashes, crimson gashes
so no slowdown could deprive
The Man of well-deserved commodity,
for had he not provided them
with home and food security?
Such prices paid to buy strong backs
who must not waste their talents on frivolity
thus service to his righteous
generosity was only due,
and God's sweet grace be his into Eternity.
Oh yes, the Grim One's ire and boundless fire,
were only what such blameless men of noble means
must do to serve divinity, and family, and country,
pockets lined so properly with silver gold prosperity.

Little one, our little girl, was growing day by day.
Each sunset brought her closer to
the night for Master's due.
Never would she feel paternal
guidance, moral and proper,
to love thy God and country,
or to champion simple kindness
to the weary of the world.
Her place in life would be a hoe,
to give their regal senior
his merited return,
the coins within his pockets,
a mansion overhead,
an aura of supremacy
provided by her toil and tears,
all delivered by that once small child,
once pretty, once playful and contented.
But now,
Stooped,
and gray,
and blistered by the sun.

She would never know
of Harriet, and Abraham, and Rosa and Martin,

for she was then so very young.

Sun rose and set then rose and set again.
Then one day it set upon her life.
Her old hoe awaited hands still too small,
but hands that would grow
and would know and would see
beyond the tower,
rotten, shameful, wicked,
beyond the fields of Grim One's searing sting.

But decades passed till noble souls
—restrained by wealth and arms—
would bleed the veins of myth.
But till that gallant stand,
little graves,
so marked by leaning, splitting oak-branch crosses,
souls forever to be gone as if
they'd never breathed or lived or cried or died.
Earthy tombs would soon be trampled
by warriors blue or gray,
their captains so resplendent
and would be honored all by statues
standing tall, *recalled* and proud.

Gone is our little girl.
Our little girl who lived and played
then toiled and wept then took her place
beneath an oak-branch cross.
Just another cross
that leaned,
then split,
then fell.

Oh Venerable Lock

by Ida Bettis Fogle

Oh venerable lock
I express my gratitude to you
every night with the ritual
turning of the cylinder.
If, in a haze of fatigue,
I forget any essential—
Tooth brushing or cat feeding—
it is not my nightly communion
with the one who will stand between
me and the forces of evil
during the time I cannot be on my own guard.
True, you are no guarantee against
all I would keep out.
A stray beetle might find its way in,
and has, along with ladybugs, spiders
and the occasional garter snake.
But so long as I have kept faithful
to the duties of the deadbolt
I have yet to find my doom
come calling.

Out of the Mouth of Babes
by Nancy Jo Cegla

For my estranged daughter

You always were an artist.
You saw what others
refused to see.

On the wall hangs a picture
you created with colored crayons
when you were but seven years-old.
It is neatly divided into two meridians.
On the left, a smiling couple walks together
with hands so tightly entwined
that they appear to be an extension
of the leash they hold.
At the end of the leash tugs a small dog
pulling them through a grove of trees
so tall that you drew white clouds
high in their leafed branches.
It is marked Reality.
The other meridian is marked Fantasy.
A smiling woman,
who has sprouted wings,
floats high above one lonely,
empty chair, and a table set with a decanter
and two glasses filled with sweet wine.
She pushes a yellow baby carriage
with orange hood and wheels
set against a clear, cloudless, blue sky;
her hands grasp a smooth carriage handle:
inside is a tiny baby.

I remember when you asked me
if I would bear your children.
The thought of carrying and delivering
a child frightened you.
Was it the pain, or the commitment?

We two spoke of intimate things
in soft, low tones.
Things that I never spoke of with your sister,
your aunt, your grandmother.
I always thought that you
could see inside me. See my
sadness like branches covered
in icy layers of snow. That, somehow, you knew.

One day, you taped a carefully scissored
poem to the inside of my computer cabinet door,
where your father would not see.
It was about what a woman should have;
what a woman should know.
It included knowing how to break up,
knowing how to live alone,
knowing who she can trust,
and knowing what she can accomplish.
Did you know the extent of my pain?

At first it was powder and lipstick
on his collars. Then his very flesh
smelled of perfume. He claimed
it was his aftershave.
He hadn't shaved since his early twenties.
And there was the painful twisting of my wrists
when we were learning conflict resolution
at your middle-school.
I used words. He could not.
He was quite proud, in the end,
that he had not hit me.

He could not speak to me,

but he did to others when I refused to stay.
He so desperately did not want
the truth to be known
that he created a fantasy from reality.
A scenario in which I starred as the betraying wife.
I foolishly chose to ignore it. Why hurt you?
Children need fathers—even fantasy fathers.

You are a part of me:
beating heart,
vulnerable flesh,
fragile mind.

You precociously knew
a woman wants to believe the fantasy.
She accepts man's seed.
She cultivates her womb.
She harvests the fruit.
She protects the children
in chariots that launch them
to soaring heights;

like migrants tending a vineyard
who do the work,
who tend the vines,
who cultivate the earth,
who harvest the fruit,
who ensure a fine vintage
to be bottled and flown high
in the skies to far away locations.

Poetic License
by Lee Ann Russell

A ballad tells a story true,
or maybe not; it's up to you.

While blank verse captures some of us,
the sonnet's work is just a plus.

Sestina, tercet, villanelle,
are formulas to learn, as well.

A cameo and short cinquain
should not be written all in vain.

A common measure gives us hymns,
and couplets make us think of twins.

While etheree has ten full lines,
a free verse poem never rhymes.

A haiku shows us nature's streak
with just three lines for us to speak.

While light verse often makes us laugh,
a limerick may prove us daft.

A tanka, triplet, triolet
or sweet vignette will have a say.

The minute captures one short time,
and all-in-all, our words are prime.

Rat Snake
by Terry Allen

My uncle yanked the black snake
out from under his old beat up truck.

It must have crawled
under there at the farm
and hitched a ride to the city

at least that's what he told us
when he came out from the house
and tried to calm my nieces
and nephews who had screamed
so loudly that you'd think someone
had been yanking on *their* tails,

but I'm here to tell you that snake
was a beauty—
six feet long
shiny black with a white belly
and small patches
of red along its sides.

Hell, he won't hurt you,
my uncle told us.
He probably crawled up there
to keep warm is all.

But the twins and my cousin Jamie
weren't buying it a bit
and were still raising hell
and hopping about like they were stepping
on a mound of fire ants.

This here's an old black snake,
my uncle said as he crouched down
a bit to try a little reason.
He helps keep the barn from being over run
by rats. That's his job.

That's when Jamie picked up a monster stick
way too big for him to handle
and the twins started bawling about
wanting to go home.

Only I suppose he can't ride
all the way back home with us,
my uncle said as he grabbed
ahold of the snake's tail
and with one mighty flick,
like he was cracking a bull whip,
he flung that snake out
and snapped its neck.

There now you kids go on
and play nice 'til lunch is ready,
my uncle said as he flung
what was left of the snake
up and into the bed of his truck.

And that was about the best
birthday party I ever had.

Red Poppies
by Nancy Jo Cegla

You told me
about the pistol,
and the shot gun
you kept at hand.
You told me
about the neighbor
who fed deer.
You told me
about the deer
that ate your flowers.
You told me
about previous disputes
with the neighbor.
You told me
he threatened harm
by poking his drunken,
bony, old finger
into your husband's
paunchy belly.
I have guns.
Ain't afraid to use 'em.
Ain't afraid to kill a man neither.
You told me
his words delivered
in a drunken slur,
on a hot day,
sent icy chills
through you.
So when I heard
about another neighbor
in yet another state

shot to death
by another husband
of another women
who encouraged
six blasts
into the neighbor's abdomen
over corn fed deer
eating flower petals
—forgive me—
I thought of you.
Your recent disputes
layered like mulch
on a flower bed,
about your children,
and your grandchildren,
and how they
would miss you.
Could colorful,
sweet and fragrant,
flowers gobbled
down to nubs on a stalk
really be that important?

So when I heard,
I pictured
a shot gun
firing snake shot
like a Tarantino scene
with blood splatter
dotting your yard
like a field
of red poppies.

Remembrance

by Barry Walker

1.
Far and apart I observed the maelstrom.
My father was a traitor, his wife, a household crone.
Their eldest son bullied into submission by jocks.
The Jesuits at school were useless gramophones of God.
This ruination I endured as the youngest.
Seething discontent burned as a mind's rage,
With only cold genius for my escape.

2.
The psychiatrist whispered promises of fur coats, jewels, and normality.
His invasive questions always asked if I was depressed.
Was it to be most of the time, some of the time, or all of the time?
This iron stew of grief was fed to my father week upon week.
Our false prosperity was spent on prep schools, job interviews, and disability checks.
I chipped away from this wreckage with pencil and paper,
Vowing a stronger will, and a freedom to come.

3.
My parents, twisted and flaying stumps, I left behind.
The midnight sky and the rising plumes of scarlet continued.
First it was to be the novel written in one semester of college,
Then came the addiction to chess, with the flurry of travel to many tournaments.
Ludendorf and Hindenborg had their Der Taug of 1918.
I would not deviate. First it would be Calais then Paris would fall.
Yet strands of bubble wrap fell away from my face.

4.

48 hours of straight work broke my father—a broken mind, a broken heart.
What Blue Cross Blue Shield owed us wasn't repaid.
The college failed to follow their blue book.
They didn't throw out B.I.G.'s men and his booming bass.
My friends and I were swapped like pawns, one suite for another.
In the new dorm I remember the probing antennae on my face.
Relentlessly I slapped, and the acrid taste of a battery followed.
The dying roach scuttled under my pillow.

    5.
I'm not sure how far I journeyed in this moonless abyss.
More pain came, my back collapsed, and then the whispers.
Acute and envious to the moaning of passion, I searched.
I pressed my ears against my neighbor's wall, and listened.
Four walls, a roof, and a new job failed to locate them.
Jimmy Hoffa and confederates yelled at me from the outside.
When I told the priest my apartment was haunted,
He only pointed at me.

Sequel
by Lee Ann Russell

Sitting on the stoop
on a sultry Summer night
watching tiny bugs
as they switch from dark to light.

Katydids are loud
as they chirp in leafy trees;
Mother Nature speaks
as she whispers in the breeze.

Summetime is here;
lovely zinnias grace the yard;
butterflies in flight
decorate the boulevard.

Autumn's on its way;
sugar maple's turning red;
Summer's buried soon
in October's leafy bed.

She Fell in Love
by Larry Allen

I fell in love with the needle
she said.
Her leg jerking rhythmically
as she spoke
it didn't matter,
meth to coke
coke to meth,
from one lover to another
searching for a substitute

I want to be normal again
she said.
A full time student
instead of a full time addict.
But I live on the edge
live for excitement
live for the needle
and that's the point.

I want to be a good mother
she said.
But lost the kids
to my junkie high
just a trophy on someone's arm
getting high
drinking beer.

It's what I am good at
she said
As she stared down
at the *crumpled papers*
in her hands….

****this is a "found poem" recorded almost word for word and spoken by a young woman during a drug counseling session. I viewed a film of the session last week and when the lady started speaking "poetry" I took out my notebook. I understand she has recovered and is doing well.****

Sherbet and Sweet, Crushed Macaroons
by Nancy Jo Cegla

My hoe spades the soil
as it has several times,
and slowly a circle appears. I
sink plants with a small hand trowel
amid the worms that surface with soil
sticking to their slimy skins. The smell
of freshly turned sod wafts through my nose.
Slim, spiky, silver leaves of the Russian Olive
filter sunlight shadowing the sheen
of beetles that move like small bulldozers.
Cicada serenades rise in the surrounding trees.

I sink the trowel into the soil again striking something
solid: a statue of St. Joseph upside down under the sod.
Forgotten after the house sold? I consider the ad
I once placed in a newspaper
for St. Jude's assistance in my despair
and loneliness. He gave compassion
to my supplications for strong arms
to encircle me on nights
that blush with starry lights bright.

Cicadas resume their sibilant sounds,
and I stand, brush off the sticky wet soil
to enter the house, and suds my hands
until squeaky clean. I shall plan a simple
dessert of sherbet. Cicada sounds bounce
off walls, ceiling and I imagine a new infestation

of these sounding bugs.
An entrepreneur once swirled blanched
and sweetened singers
into sugary frozen iced-cream
with shimmering wings
spread wide on soft scoops—
poised to escape?

But tonight I shall serve sherbet and sweet,
crushed macaroons, and sleep encircled
under blushing stars.

Thoughts After Touring the Former Missouri Penitentiary
by Ida Bettis Fogle

We used to say tools
Some still say fire
Language went out the window
With Koko the gorilla
Swans mate for life
And so do prairie voles
Jane Goodall saw chimps
Engage in a war
Violence and love and care for our young—
None of these set humans apart

But after touring the "bloodiest 47 acres"
With its cells too small
For the number sharing them
And its actual dungeon
Where men went blind
For lack of light
I could think of not another animal
That keeps its fellows captive
In such conditions for so many years
So maybe we are unique

Tonya Harding Counsels Lizzie Borden
by Larry Allen

Just go for the knees, girl,
Just go for the knees
Get a two foot length of pipe,
Skate right over and give 'em a whack.
Crack some knees and they will never
Go up those stairs again.

And get rid of that prim and proper thing.
I should know.
You can take the trash out of the trailer
But you can't park the trailer next to the trash…
Or something like that.

Try this Lizzie:
As you skate
Reach behind your back,
Pull your leg up over your head
And spin like the devil.

I don't know if that will help
But it sure as heck can't hurt.

Too Pretty
by Larry Allen

She told the officer
She was too pretty to be arrested,
But she was anyway.
Too pretty to see the judge,
Too pretty for probation.

No shrinking violet, this girl,
She was too pretty to pass a drug test.
She stood ultra close
To her male Probation Officer
Giving him free looks
So he could fully appreciate
How pretty she was.

She worked in a strip club for tips
And asked to work as an escort
So she could pay court costs.
This girl was just too pretty.
Much too pretty
For the needle marks on her arm.

Trapped
by C.A. Simonson

I am sorely trapped
I can't get out.
The walls around me
Are tall and stout.

Though they can't be seen
I cannot feel
Yet the walls remain,
Yes. They are real.

I made them myself
With bricks of pride
Unwittingly laid
Now trapped inside

I cried out to God
He knows my loss
He opened a door
Shaped like a cross.

He bids me to come,
"Come, enter in.
New life is waiting
Away from sin."

I am Freedom's Door,
The cost is free,
Just come to the cross.
Just come – to Me."

Though there all along
To set me free
Was busy building
More walls for me.

So I turned my head;
Dismissed His call,
And kept on building
My selfish walls.

Treasures
by Barbara Backes

You search the world for buried treasure following the trail,
Where "x" marks the trophy spot, you dig deep to no avail.

You travel a million miles yet find no treasure chest,
Exhausted from your journey you close your eyes to rest.

Realize as you ponder your ventures from the start,
God blesses you with abundant gifts etched inside your heart.

Dig deep within yourself search for the treasure that awaits,
Embrace your faith, your values and your distinctive traits.

Unlock and radiate your findings to the human race,
Fill the world with your wealth making it a better place.

A bounty of riches more precious than a chest of gold,
You will find within your reach to cherish and to hold.

The priceless gems of family, the treasures of a friend,
More valuable than all the gold you could ever spend.

The jewels found in nature may be smaller than a fleck of gold,
Magnify God's beauty; reveal treasures to cherish and to hold.

Before you trek mile after mile on a treasure quest,
Know the treasures within your reach are by far the best.

Vacant Save For This
by Kayla Nilges

Weekend trip. Pack his things. Rural. Small town.
Time forgot.
Open the trunk. Swirling truth.
Snapshot.
Crochet.
Sunday's best.
Babies and kisses and Christmas day.
This is what matters.
Thought abrupt.
Close the lid.
Before it sinks in.

Waiting
by Hope Longview

Out to the beach. Savor the stillness of inky darkness. Damp sand cool on bare feet. She notices the lone surf-fisher wondering. How often? From where? Why? How long? She won't ask. Can't break the silence. Wouldn't dare.

Salted-breezes cause her to wish for a sweatshirt, shivering. Distant thunderheads surf the horizon. Shades only just unmasked. Morning star pierces moonless sky. Or is that Venus?

Gunmetal hues play tag and tumble on gentle waves. Lap sand from beneath her toes. Turn to quicksilver. Recede.

If I stay, I will sink—an abandoned hull.

A pair of sandpipers arrive. Dodge sea foam. Bow and dance to the song of new day's rising.

This blessed peace, fleeting, will shatter. Soon, a million shards. Hurry urges. Blushing dawn whispers. Stay. Remember. She hugs herself. Clings to solace behind shuttered lids. Senses growing light. Waits.

The first gull's keen ruptures against the shushing wind. She smiles. Resignation nods. Shrill call, signal the ragtag masses. Come, Combers, dawdle. Joggers, slog.

We wait here groaning.
Marooned wreckage, our longing.
Tireless tide rolls on.

Your Favorite Time of Year
by Debra Sutton

This is your favorite
Time of year
Pumpkin Spice Cappuccino
And having family near

Spending lots on presents
(Just don't tell Matt)
Eating loads of food
No, you're not getting fat

Corny Christmas movies
And beautiful lights
The choir singing carols
On cold crisp nights

Shoveling snow
(For some odd reason)
Oh, how you love
The holiday season.

Can you see the snow
Through your hospital window?
And do you even know
Winter's arrived?

The doctors all say
You'll never really function
But I pray and I pray
I don't listen to them.

You're fierce and strong

Those experts don't know you
But how can they be wrong?
With their many degrees?

Because you'll never quit
For those you hold dear
And the docs don't get it
This is your favorite time of year.

Flash Fiction

2016

Maybe Next Time
by Billie Holladay Skelley

First Place

The only thing left in the bedroom is my mother's old, green chest.

As a child, I'd quizzed her repeatedly about its contents. Her clues were few: It was for me. It had never been used. I would love it.

Those were happy times, but then Mom got sick. Cancer took her on my seventeenth birthday. I didn't know what to do, so I ran off with Colton. Big mistake—because Colton ran off when he found out I was pregnant with our daughter.

So, I had to come back to our old house. At least now, I can see what the chest contains.

The lid creaks as I open it. Tissue paper is everywhere. I see white lace.

It's a wedding dress.

I do love it.

Then I realize—Mom never got to wear it. It's too late for me. I close the lid. Perhaps my daughter will.

Heaven's Gate
by Karen Mocker Dabson

The iron grillwork's cold always penetrated her fingers, but still Siobhan would cling to the black gate, ineluctably drawn. Like a hummingbird seeking the sweetest nectar, she yearned for the world beyond the filigree barricade. To brush through its tall grasses, their morning dew raining refreshment, would be heaven itself.

She slipped to the locked postern every day and for long hours, watched the windswept lea. If the groundskeeper appeared, she would slide into the shadows swiftly, silent as she had come. Sometimes he spied her and scolded, but mostly, she remained alone, undetected.

One Friday, the gate stood ajar, scarcely wider than her slim form. How she'd arrived at this forsaken place of internment remained a mystery, but now the understanding meadow invited her escape. Slipper-footed, Siobhan stepped forward. A hand grabbed her hair and yanked.

"That's quite far enough, Miss," said the orderly in his starched white coat.

You'll Get a Charge Out of This

by Frank Montagnino

Third Place

"You're going to *what?*" Deborah nearly dropped the platter she was drying. "But it's storming."

"Perfect conditions," her husband replied. "William," he shouted to his son, "bring the equipment. Hurry, lad."

William came into the kitchen loaded down with a big fabric-covered kite and a glass jar from his father's lab. "Shouldn't we wait until it stops raining?" he asked.

His father rolled his eyes. "Don't either of you understand this experiment can only be conducted when there's lightning?" He waited a beat, then blurted, "Conducted???? Don't you get it?"

Exasperated by their blank expressions he gave up and bustled out the door, dragging his son behind him. Ten seconds later he burst back into the room and removed the ornate key from the cellar door. "I'll need this for the experiment."

Deborah bustled to the door and hollered after her husband, "Ben Franklin, don't you dare lose that key."

Other Lifetimes
by Karen Mocker Dabson

Around midnight, a giant tree crashed onto the village. It smashed five houses, and its branches damaged twenty more. The mighty oak rumbled to earth, loosing a gritty fog that crept into the neighborhood. People in striped pajamas streamed from their homes, coughing and sputtering. A woman in curlers shook her head.

The mayor grabbed her robe as she ran to the scene. "Oh, God," she said, "It's the Cratchit's...*and* the Littles?" She bit her knuckles. "All this damage. We can't possibly stay now. Need somewhere new, soon."

In the attic, Posy peered into the dusty toy trunk, regretting the tiny crushed village her mother had flung there so long ago. She fingered one of the houses. It still held a trace of sand. She sighed. *Best to move on.* Closing the lid to shutter the past, she chilled as a thin, high voice piped, "Stop! It's dark in here."

Secrets Unlocked
by Amy Christianson

By the time I was four years old I knew my older sisters had secrets they shared with each other and their friends. I felt sad when they wouldn't share these secrets with me.

My oldest sister, Virginia, kept her secrets locked in her diary. It was a small, red book with a lock on a strip of binding attached to the covers holding the pages together.

One afternoon during my nap time in a bedroom upstairs, I found Virginia's treasured diary. If I could only open this book I would know her secrets. Very quietly I slipped downstairs, found scissors in the kitchen drawer and sneaked back upstairs without anyone seeing me.

I cut the strip of binding and opened the book of my sister's precious secrets. Alas, no secrets would be revealed that day! The secrets were all written in words I had not yet learned to read.

The Secret of Life
by Susannah Albert-Chandhok

Forgotten in the corner of a lonely alley, a chest protects an ancient text that reveals to its reader the secret of life. I approach the box, the color of a sickly mermaid's tail, leaving in my wake debris from years spent searching. My calloused palm cradles the bronze key. I exhale as I pierce the locks, feeling tremors from the key's teeth gnawing deeply. My arms, strengthened by imbibing my body's adrenaline liqueur, lift open the heavy top. The book bubbles up from a wave of sea foam and dust, like Aphrodite, and the fragrance of dead pages clouds me. Suddenly, with the ferocity of Zeus, the book attacks my face. I struggle as the fibers of the crinkled pages hook into my skin. I cannot exhale. Trapped between the pages, I focus my eyes on the inscribed black words: *Some secrets are not worth learning.*

The Inheritance
by Chinwe I. Ndubuka

Elvin unlocked the door and pulled the knobby key out of the keyhole. Back when Maya was a girl promising to be careful in the gigantic doll house, he kept the key so she couldn't accidentally lock herself inside. This time, he gave it to her. "It's yours."

Maya forced a smile as she eyed her grandfather's old shed in what used to be a bustling farm. Its wooden walls were tarnished blackish-brown and roofing shingles lay on the ground around them. "Why not sell it with the land? I have a garage."

"Because I want *you* to have it." He patted the structure as if it were a horse. "Some paint and nails is all it needs."

Maya pulled the handle gingerly. The door creaked open as it always had, and just as faithfully, her heart expected good. "What if I keep the key?"

"Anything for you."

The Prince
by Danyele Read

She unlocked the old wooden chest, then tilted it. Out spilled hundreds of keys.

"These are copies of all the keys to every door in every castle in the kingdom, from the master bedrooms to the butlers' quarters, to treasure rooms guarded by dragons."

Some keys were larger than my forearm, others miniscule.

"Only one opens this door. If you find it, you will succeed me as princess, well, in your case prince, of the realm. You have three tries."

"And if I don't find it?" I asked

"Then, you die, you and your family." She shrugged.

I scanned the keys. Most were rusty. Rust perhaps caused by oil from the hands of those now dead?

I took the only polished key, inserted it, and click!

She scowled.

"And you must live," I said.

"But why spare me?"

"Because," I said, "only mercy teaches true regret."

The Wedding Dress
by Amanda Booloodian

The roaring tempest reached its peak and plunged the room into darkness.

"John–"

Molly's voice died. The habit of calling out for John was ingrained after years of marriage. Only the memory of his comfort survived.

Tears stung eyes ringed with lines of bygone laughter.

John would never answer again.

Shadows of the room clutched at her heart and tied themselves to a green trunk. The ornamental filigree clashed with the stark padlocks that imprisoned the contents.

Once again she dismissed her promise to move on. Lingering memories pulled her across the room.

Molly took a tired key from its hook. Feeble knees objected as she knelt. Clasping each lock in turn, the scrape of metal on metal challenged the dying roar of wind and rain.

After tracing the path of sage slats she opened the lid. Mothball scent surged into the air. Mute, the freed contents waited.

Treasure in the Trunk
by C.A. Simonson

Rosie escaped, sobbing, to her attic hideaway devastated by cruel, hateful words. She frowned at her image in the upright mirror. *They're right. I'm ugly, fat…and unloved.* She traced the jagged scar making it swell across her cheek. *I'm cursed with the devil's kiss!*

Turning in the mirror, she caught a glint of something shiny in the back corner. Sunlight sparkled off the locks of an ancient trunk. She blew away layers of dust, unlocked it, and lifted the lid. Excited, she discovered a box with a golden shawl.

Holding it to her face, she peered into the mirror again. The shameful mark disappeared behind its softness, and Rosie felt beautiful. She smiled at the princess gazing back at her. She twirled in delight with laughter – transported to a world far from hurt. Transformed, her spirit soared. She breathed in new freedom. There was no hate here.

Wisconsin Cows
by Amy Christianson

The image of two cows grazing in a hillside pasture reminds me of my first trip to Wisconsin with my boyfriend, Jack.

We were driving through the countryside when I saw two black cows in a pasture on the side of a hill. Jack said "In Wisconsin, cow's legs are shorter on one side than they are on the other." He went on to explain that cows always walk the same way around a hill so in time the downhill legs become longer and the uphill legs become shorter.

In Freshman biology class we learned that people and animals adapt to environmental conditions so this sounded logical to me. Later when I met Jack's aunt I mentioned I didn't know about Wisconsin cows until today. When she laughed and pointed at Jack I realized I'd been had. In spite of this deception, I married him anyway.

In 100 words or less write a Flash Fiction Story or Flash Fiction Poem that starts with a famous quote and ends with the words "So be it."

Do Not Disturb
by Hope Longview

"What I like doing best is Nothing."–A.A. Milne, Winnie-the-Pooh

Dr. Evans opened her clutch and placed the paperweight etched with her favorite childhood quote on the bedside table of her Four Seasons New York suite. She unplugged all the clocks and posted the do-not-disturb sign. Then, she changed into her new silk pajamas and ordered an expensive merlot and the petit filet from room service.

"You'll be dead in less than a month—two tops." David, her colleague and oncologist had said.

Thankful for his frankness, she replied, "So be it."

Backwards and in High Heels
by Susan Koenig

"Sure he was great, but don't forget that Ginger Rogers did everything he did,...backwards and in high heels." Hillary quoted the *Frank and Ernest* comic strip she had taped to the refrigerator years before.

Bill pursed his lips and nodded without looking up from his book, *An Inconvenient Truth*.

Hillary set aside her phone which displayed a chart of the current odds of a woman becoming president, forwarded by Bill earlier in the day. They both knew too well the financial and emotional price tag.

"I'm going to run."

He looked up and replied, "So be it."

Life with Mother
by Lori Younker

If life gives you lemons, make lemonade. I rehearse the saying slicing lemons in half.

"How about lemonade?" I hunt for the juicer in the cupboard next to the sink.

"We just had some," Mother responds.

"That was a week ago," I say, shoulders tensing.

"What did you ask me?"

Here we go again.

"Do you want some lemonade?"

I twist and smash the lemons against the surface of the juicer, watch the liquid accumulate in the jar beneath.

"Some what?"

"Lemonade," I say.

"Something smells good," she says.

Conversation isn't what it used to be. So be it.

In 150 words or less, write a Flash Fiction Story or Flash Fiction Poem set in a time period other than the present.

The Queue
by Julie Pimblett

I had on all of the clothes I had brought and still the wind chilled me as it whistled through the cavernous building sending the black and brown scarves of the hundreds of people in line twirling. We shifted position backing away from the wind but careful to maintain our places in the queue.

Two weeks at sea to get here. The pungent vinegary smell of urine still clung to our muddy shoes. No one smiled. After all this time we were still not here. Those at the front got dismissed for reasons none of us behind could fathom. I inched closer watching the doctors chalk "L" on the people being turned away. I pulled my shawl closer holding off the organisms that might return me to the horror of life outside of here. The stethoscope was freezing through my shirt. The doctor nodded. I was free.

Out of Time
by Rexanna Ipock-Brown

Running late, Lisa turned off the radio. Regan had not been her choice for president. Car parked, she headed into the restaurant and located her friends.

"Are you ready for the spicy noodles?" asked Ricki, her hair a sculpture of gel and spray.

"Nah, just sour soup and salad. I like living long and healthy more than noodles." Lisa scooted in her chair.

"Live a little now." Marcia's chair made a scraping noise as she bounced to the table. The mule she had tie-dyed on her tee shirt nodded in agreement as her chest sprang up and down with her effort.

"I might take a bite of yours."

Marcia grinned. "Anytime."

Sated with the food and company, they headed home.

"See you next Thursday?" Lisa asked.

"Same place," said Ricki.

"Same time," said Marcia.

Lisa's last thought as the drunk t-boned her car was I should have had the noodles.

Twisted Together
by Hope Longview

Today, of all days, Marietta wished she wasn't so clumsy. The children in school teased her behind her back because her left hand curled into a fist and her twisted left leg kept her from running after them. She was 23 years old and had finally reconciled herself to life as a spinster schoolmarm when Willie Honeycut asked to step out with her. Willie had inherited his father's feed store and thought having a book-learnt wife would do him some good. He even said she was mighty pretty for a schoolmarm. Her granny, a Baptist Sunday School teacher, crossed herself and praised the Holy Mother. Marietta didn't mind that Willie's left arm had been shot off in the great war. Now, she could see him waiting at the altar. She held tight to Pappy's arm and walked as straight as she was able toward her grinning groom.

Research in Seattle
by Liz Davis

Pulling into a parking space at KCI, I looked around for Eve.

Thump! My car jarred like something from outer space had landed on it. Which it had, I thought with a smile.

I got out and locked my car.

Eve opened her car door and looked down at me. "Why don't you ever park with an empty space next to you?"

"Quit complaining," I said climbing up and into the passenger seat. "I need to be back in a couple of hours."

"Sure, no problem. I'll drop you in Seattle while I interview the witness in LA. We'll be home in plenty of time for dinner."

Eve put the car in vertical lift and we were off.

In 200 words or less, write as Flash Fiction Story or Flash Fiction Poem that uses the Albert Einstein quote: "When you are courting a nice girl an hour seems like a second. When you sit on a red-hot cinder a second seems like an hour. That's relativity."

A Relative Quote
by Carrie Koepke

"When you are courting a nice girl an hour seems like a second. When you sit on a red-hot cinder a second seems like an hour. That's relativity."

Jamie Sayen's pen flew. "And Professor Einstein said that?"

Helen Dukas dipped her head with a false shyness. Everyone always wanted to know what Albert said, but they never understood a damn word. She wondered how to make him look at her – for an hour that seemed like a second. "Essentially. I'd be happy to explain it further, but the Professor is busy." Helen looked from the closed door to the reporter pointedly.

Jamie thought about mentioning that he and Albert were neighbors, that he could talk to him anytime, but then he would have no excuse to leave the musty university, to stand close to a pretty girl, to see her flip her hair as he peeked over the spiral binding of his notebook. "Perhaps you could tell me more," Jamie tried to look cool as he turned his watch face upward, "over lunch?"

Helen smiled. A Princeton boy. Albert always was telling her to date someone smart enough to hold his own. "Lunch sounds nice."

It's All Relative

by Julie Pimblett

"When you are courting a nice girl an hour seems like a second. When you sit on a red-hot cinder a second seems like an hour. That's relativity." Fat lot of good that does me now. A head full of quotes doled out to the unwashed and uninterested seems like a pretty wasted life. Doesn't matter, does it? Everyone's life is wasted in the end, isn't it? We all come to this. Time has slowed down now. The preparations are taking place. Ah, so that's why that quote just popped into my head. Freud wasn't so far wrong, the old unconscious works overtime.

The bitch had it coming anyway. Sitting there crossing her legs all basic-instinct style with those tight short skirts and that smirk. She knew just what she was doing. Those little gropes in the hallway and then the big number on that old couch in my office; dust leaping from it as we rutted away. The blackmail. My reputation. My marriage. My tenure. Bitch. She had it coming. I could've done a better job of it if I'd planned it. How could the jury think it was first degree, couldn't they see a man like me would've planned it a lot better? Stupid shits. My peers, yeah that's rich. How fucking long does it take to put on three straps for god's sakes? Seems like forever. I guess it is, isn't it? Hah! A joker till the end. Put the damn needle in will ya'?

It's All Relative
by Debra Sutton

"'When you are courting a nice girl an hour seems like a second. When you sit on a red-hot cinder a second seems like an hour. That's relativity.' Albert Einstein said that."

My brother-in-law rubbed lotion on my sister's mostly unresponsive arms. It was no secret Matt liked to talk, and he'd never met a story he couldn't tell, but ever since Margie's complications due to a brain tumor, his cheerfulness was slightly forced and the crinkles around his eyes a little worn.

I wasn't sure if he was making a point or just conversation, but I had to agree with Matt and Albert. Although it'd only been a few months since Margie had fallen into a coma-like state, it seemed like years since I'd heard her infectious laugh.

The doctors were hopeful, stating there was no reason she couldn't come out of it. Every day brought progress. And the first movement of her fingers as she'd touched her daughter's head incited cheering as if she'd ran a marathon.

"Maybe so," I said, squeezing Margie's curled fingers. "But after all that snow shoveling, when she finally comes out of it and realizes she missed summer, she's gonna be *relatively* pissed."

In 250 words or less, write a Flash Fiction Story or Flash Fiction Poem using all five senses: taste, touch, smell, sight and sound.

I Bless the Rains
by Hope Longview

The sun breaks through thunderheads
Spotlighting the huge jacaranda tree.

Her blooming halo shimmers—
Polished amethyst. Fallen petals glitter—
a purple ring against the dark wet earth.

I, alone, glimpse the Tree of Life and
Gape, unblinking, as angels sing,
"Worthy is the Lamb!"

Chocolatey delusions of grandeur subsume me.

Glorious jacaranda shaped confection!
I envision flourless dark chocolate cake
Layered with smooth rich ganache.
I'll pour glaçage. Sculpt fondant.
Tree trunk and limbs unfurl—waiting.
Spin delicate blossoms—glistening.
Violet and indigo—sugar glass gems.
Aroma of premium cacao, envelop me!
Espresso-laced, palate perfection! Mmmm!

Mere milliseconds. Clouds collapse. Glory gone.

I startle, stuporous, wedged deep in a matatu minibus.
Designed for fourteen, we carry eighteen, plus
Kids and cargo—the sofa on top paid extra.

I've gone noseblind to the stench of humanity,
But remain overwhelmed by acrid diesel fumes,
and the reek of wet goat.

Forced onto my lap, a sobbing toddler pees himself—
His warm urine soaks my leg and boots. Eventually,
They disembark—the toddler, his mum, her goat.

Two men squeeze in, shoving me further
Against the window. Furtive hands explore
My pockets, unfazed at finding toddler-soaked lint.

Filth encircles mean roadside shanties.
Ragged babies suckle hollow-eyed mothers.
World without end.

Pray. Focus. Breathe.
In—Three more hours…
Out—Please, help me endure…
In—Three more hours…
Out—Grant me sugary hallucinations…

1 November 2006:
From Nyahururu to Nairobi:
    -Antimalarials *also* cause wicked daydreams.
    -Remember fiery jacaranda.
    -Buy chocolate.

Untitled

by Kathy Kelley

What the hell is it this time Marjorie?

Don't cuss Leonard, God is always listening.

I doubt that Marjorie. I have asked him repeatedly to get rid of our obnoxious neighbor, but he's still here. Damn it Marjorie! It smells like cat urine in here.

Oh, stop it Leonard! I bought some curtains today. They are vintage barkcloth. I got a great deal on them. Look Leonard.

I see them Marjorie.

Now come here Leonard and just run your hand over this fabric. They don't make curtains like this anymore Leonard. Here, feel it.

No thank you Marjorie. I can smell it, that's enough. Here's an idea, why don't you wash them?

Leonard, you can't wash this vintage fabric, it could shrink. They're a little musty from being in storage.

Then they must have stored them in a litter box. Take them to the dry cleaners Marjorie.

Don't be silly Leonard. It will cost more to dry clean them, then I paid for them. Besides, I heard that's very bad for the environment. I'll just spray them with Febreze.

Then they'll smell like cinnamon-infused urine Marjorie.

Sit down Leonard, your show is on and the pot pie just dinged in the microwave.

I won't be able to taste my food with that smell in here Marjorie. You know how sensitive my stomach is. Where are the curtains that were here this morning?

I threw them out Leonard. They were old.

Older than vintage?

Relax, I'll get you a beer.

OK.

Memories

by Debra Kaye Sutton

The wood creaked beneath her feet as Emma explored the attic cluttered with so many forgotten things. It was there. It had to be. Her grandma's final words, whispered brokenly, promised it. As her eyes adjusted to the light, Emma pushed back memories of Sunday mornings curled next to her grandma's old rocker listening to vivid stories somehow untouched by age. She could almost smell the homemade oatmeal cookies served with tea, that as a child made her feel special and loved. Now barely eighteen, Emma wasn't ready to let go of that feeling. Or her grandma.

The salty taste of her tears reminded her of why she was there. She was on a mission. Pushing past a box of long forgotten Christmas ornaments and broken knickknacks, she finally reached her goal.

Relief welled up in her chest at the sight of the old steam trunk looking just as her grandma described it. Her fingers traced the worn scratches, the feel of each eliciting sadness and excitement in equaling measures, sharpening the pain of her loss, and yet driving her forward. Inside were her grandmother's memories, those stories Emma loved so much, brought to life.

Her fingers trembled as she lifted the key from around her neck and slid it into the lock.

She didn't know why her grandma had waited until after her death to share this with her. But as she clicked the locks open, and lifted the lid, she realized …

She was about to find out.

Flash Fiction
Time Capsule Contest

Congratulations to **Suzanne Connelly Paulter** for winning the Flash Fiction Time Capsule Contest, in which writers were asked to depict life in Missouri 50 years from now. Also congratulations to close runner-up **Debbie Sutton**.

The time capsule is a project of the Missouri Arts Council, the state agency supporting arts in Missouri. The locked steel box will be stored in the MAC offices in the Old Post Office in St. Louis, at 815 Olive Street.

Suzanne's and Debbie's works will be stored in a time capsule to be open in June 2066. Both will also appear in Well Versed.

Interviews and bios of both will accompany the winning entries and will appear on the Columbia Chapter of the Missouri Writers Guild website.

WINNER

Simple Livin' - June 25, 2066
by Suzanne Connelly Pautler

Good boy, Freddy. Hold still now while I get those burrs out, then we'll walk to the pond. Just my old bird dog and me.

Sky sure is blue and the hills are showin' off their splendid green. Beautiful.

Hear the geese? Flyin' low today.

Yep, things haven't changed much 'round here for ol' Uncle David. One hundred years in this fine Missouri countryside and still here to enjoy it. Who would o' thought? Simple livin' does it for me. Sure, modern ways cured my cancer, fixed my heart, and keeps my ol' body workin', but this country life's what really keeps me goin'. They'll see I'm right when they get here. They'll be here soon.

The ducks sure look peaceful, ripplin' the water so. And smell that fresh air.

Don't need new gadgets out here to keep me happy. Never had a fancy phone, smart they called 'em. Didn't fall for computers either. All gatherin' dust now, along with smart cars, parts of smart kitchens, smart glasses, even those fancy smart clothes. Now, 'cordin' to the ads, Marveltec homes and accessories, "work marvelously through your thoughts." They say they only have to think and, Voila, lights turn on, doors open, coffee brews, and to beat it all, their feelins' are evaluated and little spray whatevers puff around their houses to calm them. What's the world comin' to?

We get along just fine with the soothin' hum of crickets and usin' my God given hands and fingers to turn knobs and switches, open doors, and prepare food. Yes, sir, and I'll keep my country home any day, with only its basic '46 Zephyrphone to meet communication requirements.

Sun's gettin' high. See anyone yet? Don't need those implanted vision enhancers and supersonic hearin' doodads, just my good ol' lasered eyes and hearin' devices.

You know they say they can't live without modern doohickeys? Hogwash. Why not walk, bike, and run? Take a walk in the woods, like man did for centuries. Without their aerial aerobic thingamajigs, their bodies would turn to mush. And what's the youth comin' to today? Hardly leavin' their homes anymore.

See that, Freddy? In the eastern sky? Here they come, way out from the city. Must be a dozen of 'em in their colorful Celopods. Word sounds like a dinosaur, huh. Beats me why they can't come on the ground anymore.

I'll wait 'til they're closer to light it. More dramatic that way. One, two, three... Hee haw, there it goes. Good ol' fashioned gasoline to light this huge bonfire. Bet they haven't seen that before.

They're droppin' out of the sky like flies.

Guess now that the relatives are here my one hundredth birthday party can begin.

Suzanne Connelly Pautler started dabbling with writing during her childhood years in the 1960s and 1970s while growing up in both St. Louis, then in rural Franklin County, Missouri. She is an avid reader, nature lover, historical presenter, and genealogy detective. As a life-long learner, she enjoys researching a variety of topics, particularly those related to history. Suzanne and her husband reside in Columbia, Missouri and have three grown children.

1. What's most important in your life in 2016?

Family is most important to me in 2016. I value my time with my husband and our immediate and extended family. The little ones are so entertaining and great at giving hugs. The older members hold a special place in my heart. I also enjoy capturing family stories through recording their experiences.

2. If you could keep one aspect of 2016 the same in 2066, what would it be?

I would keep kindness to others in 2066. Many people in my lifetime and before, have shown great kindness and helpfulness to others near them and around the world. I feel that by turning our thoughts away from ourselves, we make the world a better place now and for the future.

3. Where do you see technology in 2066?

I see less "gadgets" or technological devices in 2066. We've come a long way with smart phones, as this one item performs many tasks that used to be completed by separate items. I predict people will have ways to perform tasks and receive information that take up very little space and won't need to be held. For transportation, I imagine that an option for everyday travel will be a vehicle in the air. As far as medical technology, I hope and pray that medical advancements will progress to the point that there will be cures for all cancer, diabetes, heart disease, and many, or all, diseases.

4. List three things you would like Missourians to know about the year 2016?

1) Nature abounds and Missouri is beautiful! Due to insightful people of the past and present, we enjoy many natural areas to walk, hike, bicycle, canoe, camp, spelunk, fish, hunt, birdwatch, see wild animals, and more.

2) Religion is an important part of many people's lives and places of worship are common in Missouri towns and cities.

3) Missouri has a diverse population, particularly in larger cities. Main areas of diversity include racial, socioeconomic, religious, and educational. Among these areas, racial equality continues to be a pressing issue. Recently, groups have spoken out for and improvements have been made toward racial equality, particularly in the areas of law enforcement and on college campuses.

5. If you had a magic wand and could have anything you wanted for 2066, what would it be?

I would want people to honor the people and history of the past, to preserve natural resources and live peaceably, kindly, and honestly with each other, and to prepare young people for the future.

SECOND PLACE

A Change in Time
By Debbie Sutton

Tui engaged the automatic feature on her Prius as she leaned back, sipping the cappuccino she swiped that morning. She rubbed her wrist, knowing the implant was buried too far in to feel but unable to stop the reflex. A quick scan could pay for her coffee, prove her identity, or provide her complete medical history. No need to even carry a purse like her great-grandmother used to do.

As her car slowed to a mere seventy, she glanced down at the road with concern. The speed limit on the windy roads was a hundred, and it was double that on the interstates. If she was slowing down, something must be tipping the sensors off. As she zoomed over the hill, she could see a large horse pulling a black buggy along the side of the road. She manually slowed the car down even more to avoid scaring the horse and driver. It amazed her that in this day and age the Amish still stayed true to their beliefs, like they had for hundreds of years.

After passing the old-fashioned vehicle, she used the opportunity to gaze at the fields, watching the majestic combines zip the corn from the ground, harvesting the fields within minutes. As a kid, Tui loved watching the sun bounce off the force fields on her daddy's farm. They were not only colorful, but they also shielded the crops from the elements and provided extra rain when needed. Losing crops was a thing of the past, and because of that most everyone in the world had plenty to eat.

Of course, life wasn't perfect by any means. They still had corruption, since there was always be greedy people to be found. Identity theft was an especially heinous crime. She shuddered at some of the things she'd heard about and rubbed her wrist again.

But, overall things seemed better than in her great-grandmother's day.

She engaged the speed button once again, anxious to get to her job at the conservation office. Protecting animals and the environment had always been her passion and recent advancements in science and technology made it an exciting time to be a biologist. As the countryside zipped by in a colorful blur, Tui was thankful she lived in Missouri with its stunning cities and rich heartlands. That was one thing that would never change.

Debra K Sutton is a dedicated social worker and author. By day, she works as a Specialist for the Children's Division through the State of Missouri. She has a Bachelor's of Arts in Psychology from Truman University and a Master's of Social Work from the University of Missouri—Columbia. All of her other free time (not spent with family and friends) is focused on writing. Her debut novel, Broken Sidewalks, has received favorable reviews. Her second novel is due to be released in 2016.

1. What's most important in your life in 2016?

My family, including my children: Ryan, Tristan, and Katie; my daughter-in-law Shandra; my sisters: Jan, Jackie, Kelly, and Margie; and my brother Curt; and my dad.
My friends, including work friends, old friends, writing friends, and church friends.
My church.
The support I've received from all has been a blessing.
My treasures are my grandchildren, Tyler and Samantha.

2. If you could keep one aspect of 2016 the same in 2066, what would it be?

The beauty of Missouri ... in fact, I'd like to preserve the whole world. As we make technological advances, it seems the environment is the thing that suffers the most. We need to care for our planet and the animals that cohabit it with us.

3. Where do you see technology in 2066?

Besides the things I've listed in my flash fiction piece, I see interactive holograms as being fairly common in 2066, taking Facetime to a whole new level.

4. List three things you would like Missourians to know about the year 2016?

   1) Our president in 2016, Barack Obama, has made great progress over the last seven years with very little support. He did it with grace and humor, and I think

history will look favorably upon him, even if much of the country did not.

2) Leonardo DiCaprio finally won an Oscar, and it was a big deal.

3) Many legends died this year already including, David Bowie, Alan Rickman, and Glenn Frey, and we're only three months in.

5. If you had a magic wand and could have anything you wanted for 2066, what would it be?

If I had a magic wand and could have anything I wanted for 2066, I think I would want to have remarkable advancements made in the study of the brain. The brain is unchartered territory, at least according to the neurosurgeons working with my sister, Margie. She had blood clots go to her lung after surgery, causing her to suffer brain damage. If we could really harness the amazing power of the brain, especially in the areas of biofeedback, things like brain injuries, cancer, diabetes, strokes, and other ailments and conditions could possibly be repaired by our bodies and minds.

Appendices

Appendix A: Contributors

Albert-Chandhok, Susannah

Susannah Albert-Chandhok is originally from New Orleans, Louisiana. She graduated from Yale College in 2014 with her degree in psychology. She currently lives in Columbia, MO and has two cats, Athena and Yoshimi.

Allen, Larry

Larry W. Allen has had poems published in *Main Street Rag, The Hatchet, Mid America Poetry Review, Boston Literary Magazine, Fine Arts Discovery* and other publications. His book, *Do Come in and Other Lizzie Borden Poems* was published by Pear Tree Press. Larry is a retired probation officer who lives in Columbia Missouri.

Allen, Terry

Terry Allen lives in Columbia, Missouri and is an Emeritus Professor of Theatre Arts at the University of Wisconsin-Eau Claire, where he taught acting, directing and playwriting. He directed well over a hundred plays during his thirty-eight years of teaching. A few favorites include: Candide, Macbeth, Death of a Salesman, and The Threepenny Opera. He now writes poetry and has been published in Fine Arts Discovery, Well Versed, I-70 Review, Freshwater Poetry Journal, Boston Literary Magazine, Garbanzo Literary Journal, Bop Dead City, Third Wednesday, Whirlwind Magazine, Star 82 Review, and Modern Poetry Quarterly Review.

Backes, Barbara

Barbara Backes enjoys writing poetry in her spare time. She has had poems published in *The Catholic Missourian, 2015 Immaculate Conception Church Directory and Well Versed.* Barbara works with children on a daily basis as an After School Care Director and part time elementary Art teacher. She is co-owner of Treasured Keepsakes. She also enjoys spending time with her husband, children and grandchildren.

Baum, Pablo

Pablo returned to Oklahoma in 1976 after nine years of adventurous graduate studies (Colombia, Puerto Rico, Mexico) with Colombian wife Consuelo and then moved to Missouri in 1979 to raise Tica and Glen.

Studies in linguistics and folklore inspire him to embrace *los de abajo (those at the bottom)* which permeate his storytelling and writings to this day.

Boes, Brianna

Brianna has been a writer all her life, but it took a little bit of life experience for her to realize writing was a true passion she wanted to pursue. She is a mother to two beautiful children, and wife to one of the most amazing and supportive husbands one could find. With family, faith, and writing, her life is full to the brim, and she wouldn't have it any other way.

Booloodian, Amanda

Amanda Booloodian currently works in K-12 Virtual Education. She has been passionate about the written word most of her life. Much of her spare time is spent at the keyboard, lost in worlds accessible only through vivid imagination. Most often she can be found staring into space or wandering the woods, but a good plot twist or discussion on writing will bring her around.

Cegla, Nancy Jo

Nancy Jo Cegla was born and raised in south Minneapolis, lived in Wisconsin for nearly thirty-four years owning and operating small businesses about thirty of those years. She is a mother of two grown daughters and grandmother to one grandson. She holds a B.A. degree from University of Wisconsin-Eau Claire, an M.F.A. in Writing (emphasis in playwriting) from Spalding University-Louisville, Kentucky, and an Associate of Applied Science from Herzing University-Crystal, Minnesota. She served as a student editor for The Louisville Review, won first place in the 2007, Metroversity Kentuckian Fiction Writing Contest. Nancy's plays have received readings at both the Playwrights' Center in Minneapolis, and the Actors Theatre of Louisville in Kentucky. In recent years her enrollment in poetry courses at The Loft has sparked a desire for further exploration of expression through poetry. Two examples of Nancy's work in both poetry and short fiction appear in Well Versed Literary Journal, 2015 edition.

Christianson, Amy

After joining CCMWG in 1997, Amy served as editor of "The Write Stuff" for two years and began collecting copies of Well-Versed. She enjoys reading and listening to stories people write about their families, their travels and adventures. Eight years ago Amy began facilitating Writers' Circle, a group that meets weekly to discuss current events and share the stories, memories and poems they have created.

Coffman, James H.

Jim is a student and writer of poetry. He is a retired minister. One of his greatest joys comes from his throwing of words together and listening to them bounce into one another. He lives with wife, Jan, his strongest supporter.

Crabtree, Maril

Maril Crabtree writes and edits in Kansas City, where she serves as board member of The Writers Place. Her most recent chapbook is *Tying the Light* (Finishing Line Press). Her work also appears in journals including *Kalliope*, *I-70 Review*, *Coal City Review*, *Main Street Rag*, *Persimmon Tree*, *Third Wednesday*, and *2014 Poet's Market*. She previously served as poetry editor for *Kansas City Voices*. More of her work can be seen at www.marilcrabtree.com.

Crawford, Peg

Peg lives, writes and draws inspiration from her own little piece of heaven just outside of Columbia Missouri. Having set aside writing to raise two fantastic kids, she recently picked up the pen again and is enjoying herself immensely.

Dabson, Karen Mocker

Karen Mocker Dabson is an award-winning author who writes novels, short stories, poems, and non-fiction. In 2015, her novel, *The Muralist's Ghost*, received second place in the Missouri Writers Guild's Walter Williams award for a major work of high literary quality and was featured in the *Pittsburgh Post-Gazette*. Her stories and poems have appeared in the CCMWG and Mozark Press anthologies, and the Story Circle journal. Karen lives in Durham, North Carolina with her husband, Brian, and Jack-the-Dog.

Faulkner, Jessica

Jessica Faulkner is a retired high school Spanish teacher of 23 years from a little burg in Ohio called Shiloh. At this junction in her life, she is excited about reviving from childhood, her love for the written word; poetry being her preference for its freedom and flexibility of expression and interpretation.

Fogle, Ida Bettis

Ida Bettis Fogle is Kansas City Royals fan who never stopped believing. She lives in Columbia, Missouri with various family members: human, feline and other. Her writing has appeared in various anthologies and literary magazines, including *Uncertain Promise* and *Well Versed*. She regularly writes for the Daniel Boone Regional Library blog *DBRL Next*.

Ipock-Brown, Rexanna

Rexanna Ipock-Brown uses her experiences as a professional psychic, hypnotist, and educator to inspire her writing. With a B.F.A. in Speech and Theater, she also is certified to teach the same, plus English. Her poetry has appeared in *Peace* magazine and her fiction, non-fiction, and flash fiction have appeared in *Well Versed*. Her first paranormal romance novel is being considered for publication. She is a member of a Romance Writers of America, Passionate Ink, Romance and More Critique Group, and the Columbia Chapter of Missouri Writer's Guild.

Koenig, Susan

Susan Koenig writes short stories and novels drawn from her cluttered imagination and life in Indiana and Missouri. She enjoys time spent with her son and lives in Columbia, Missouri with her husband.

Lawless, Andrea

Andrea Lawless is a former copywriter and ESL instructor. Originally from St. Louis, she earned a BA at Mizzou where she studied theatre and English. After teaching English in South Korea for several years, she moved back to St. Louis before finally settling down in Columbia, MO. She works as a grants administrator at the University of Missouri and has a lovely family of 1 husband, 3 kids, a cat, and a dog.

Longview, Hope

Hope Longview has been writing stories, essays and poems since she was a young girl. The busyness of her career years left little time for creative writing. Recently, a slower pace has reignited her creative writing. She's an eager traveler and eclectic reader who also enjoys classic, foreign and art house cinema. She resides near Columbia, Missouri where a dog named Boo allotters her to share his home.

McIntosh, Lynn Strand

Lynn McIntosh is a woman who is generally behind in most things. Among those are: dieting; as she is currently trying to lose the baby fat from her grandchildren, cleaning; her dust bunnies are in their sixth generation, and fashion; her push up bra is just keeping them off the floor. She writes about life and the humor she sees in it, even when no one else shares her vision. She has lived in Columbia for over thirty years and raised five sons and a husband there. Humor abounds.

Montagnino, Frank

Frank Montagnino is a retiree who spends his days cleaning house, ironing and otherwise being a perfect husband. When unchained, he flees to the golf course or huddles at the computer writing weird stories and caustic submissions to Trib Talk. If you're reading this, it means one of his writings made it into the Anthology. He hopes you enjoy it.

Ndubuka, Chinwe

Chinwe I. Ndubuka's flash fiction works have been published in *Interpretations I* and *Interpretations II*, anthologies of paired literary and visual works selected by the Columbia Art League. Another won a themed flash fiction contest organized by the Daniel Boone Regional Library. Chinwe I. Ndubuka writes from Missouri where she also works in environmental science.

Nielsen, Sheree K.

Sheree K. Nielsen, a multi-genre award winning writer and

photographer, loves the wind in her hair and the sand between her toes. In April 2015, she won the Da Vinci Eye Award for her 'healing' coffee table book, Folly Beach Dances, inspired by the sea. Publications include AAA Southern Traveler, AAA Midwest Traveler, Missouri Life, countless anthologies, newspapers, and websites. When not writing, she's usually riding around town with two goofy dogs, sipping cappuccinos. www.beachdances.com and www.shereenielsen.wordpress.com

Nilges, Kayla

Kayla Nilges is a mother, librarian, and Missouri native. Growing up in the hills of Osage County nourished her imagination, spurring a love of the written word. She has written pieces for the Columbia Art League Interpretations Show, and freelanced for *The Jefferson City News Tribune*. On weekends, Kayla can be found walking with her son, barbecuing with family, and scribbling in a notebook. Writing is, and always has been, her favorite impulse.

Paulter, Suzanne

Suzanne Connelly Pautler started dabbling with writing during her childhood years in the 1960s and 1970s while growing up in both St. Louis, then in rural Franklin County, Missouri. She is an avid reader, nature lover, historical presenter, and genealogy detective. As a life-long learner, she enjoys researching a variety of topics, particularly those related to history. Suzanne and her husband reside in Columbia, Missouri and have three grown children.

Pimblett, Julie

On behalf of the Columbia Chapter of the Missouri Writers' Guild, we would like to thank everyone who contributed to this year's edition of Well Versed and businesses for their kind support of local authors and the writing community.

Pittman, Von

Von Pittman was a flunky at several state universities until he wisely retired. His stories have appeared in *Cantos*, *Crime and Suspense*, *Cuivre River Review*, *Perspectives Magazine*, *Well Versed*, and *Iowa History Illustrated*, as well as several regional anthologies. He is building a collection of photos of manhole covers.

Read, Danyele

Danyele Read writes inspirational fiction and poetry. Her latest published novella is Hope's Motel, a modern southern romance. She is a New Yorklahoman currently residing in Texas. Learn more about Danyele and her work at www.DanyeleRead.com.

Rechenberg, Mary Koeberl

Mary Koeberl Rechenberg is a retired teacher who resides near Pocahontas, Missouri. She enjoys writing children's stories, essays, and poetry. Her work has been published in a variety of magazines, newspapers, and anthologies. Her hobbies include collecting antiques, quilting, sewing, and reading. However, spending time with her grandchildren takes priority. Her experiences while growing up on a farm have been a powerful influence in her writing.

Ridenour, Eva

Eva Ridenour has served as President of CCMWG twice and in almost every office as well as is past-treasurer of MWG. She has published nine romance novels as well as her family and hometown histories and numerous articles. Her book *Libby* received the MWG Walter Williams Award in 2005 and honorable mention for her hometown history in 2006. Recently she has concentrated on poetry published in *Mid-America Review*, *Well-Versed* and *Cappers*.

Russell, Lee Ann

Lee Ann Russell, Springfield, MO, is a member of Missouri Writers' Guild and Poets & Friends. She is past president and

Honorary Life Member of Springfield Writers' Guild, HLM of Missouri State Poetry Society, a member of the Missouri Writers' Guild, a member of the Poets Roundtable of Arkansas, and a member of Poets and Friends. She received myriad awards for poetry, prose and photography and published in numerous magazines, newspapers and anthologies. She is the author of *How to Write Poetry*, and her poem, "Last Call," won 7th place out of 2,700 *Writer's Digest* contest entries.

Salter, Kit

Kit Salter had his schooling in more than a dozen public schools—through a very mobile growing up—and went to Oberlin College and the University of California at Berkeley for college and graduate work. He spent a lot of time hitchhiking and became fascinated with how quickly life can change from ride to ride and place to place. Writing and geography seemed to be a good way to capture this variety.

Seabaugh, Laura

Laura Seabaugh grew up in the arctic winters of Green Bay, Wisconsin, where she learned to use both writing and art to take glimpses into other worlds, and never grew out of playing pretend. She works in Jefferson City as a graphic designer, and lives with her husband, their two daughters, a 15-pound cat, and one-pound chinchilla.

Simonson, C.A.

C.A. Simonson has been a writer since she was a small girl dreaming up stories. Her first publication came at age 17 with a poem. Bitten, this was a starting point in a writing career. She has written numerous nonfiction articles for magazines, newsletters, and online blogs, written three novels in the *Journey Home* trilogy, and published a short story anthology from writers all over the world. Her award-winning stories are published in five anthologies.

Siracusa, Diane

Diane moved to Hollister, MO from a lifetime spent in the Chicago suburbs. She has degrees in Media Writing and Special Education and has written free-lance articles and stories for newspapers and magazines. She maintains a recipe blog: foodmemories.net. Diane is also a portrait artist who works in pen-and-ink and colored pencil. She taught adult art lessons privately and for the Branson Arts Council. She belongs to the Springfield Writers' Guild and was Director-at-Large, 2015.

Skelley, Billie Holladay

Billie Holladay Skelley is a registered nurse who received her bachelor's and master's degrees from the University of Wisconsin in Madison, Wisconsin. She has written several health-related articles for both professional and lay journals.

Since her retirement from nursing, Billie has enjoyed focusing more on her writing, and her articles, stories, poetry, and essays have appeared in several magazines, journals, and anthologies in print and online. She has also written books for children.

Sutton, Debra

Deb Sutton is a social worker by day, and enjoys using those skills to infuse life into her characters. Her debut novel, Broken Sidewalks, is published under the name D.K. Sutton and has received positive reviews. Her second novel is scheduled for release in the spring. She's a youngish grandmother which keeps her in touch with her inner child. Besides writing, she enjoys crocheting, reading mysteries with a side of romance, and collecting elephants.

Wahler, Pat

Pat Wahler is a recently retired grant writer living near St. Louis with her husband and an assortment of pets. She is an award winning writer with multiple publications in the Chicken Soup for the Soul anthologies, Cup of Comfort anthologies, Sasee Magazine, and numerous other publications. Pat draws inspiration from family, friends, and the critters who tirelessly supervise every moment she spends at the keyboard.

Walker, Barry, PhD

Dr. Walker got his doctorate in biochemistry and currently works for ABC Labs. He enjoys wargaming, chess, writing, swimming, and learning. Science-fiction and fantasy novels are his primary focus in writing.

Younker, Lori

Lori Younker enjoys teaching reading and writing to young English language learners at the elementary level. Her life is rich with friends from all over the world and celebrates all things cross-cultural. At the heart of her writing is lessons learned while living with her family in Mongolia, causes worth fighting, and poking fun at herself.

Appendix B: Columbia Chapter of the Missouri Writer's Guild

Board:
President: Lori Younker
Vice President: Debra Sutton
Secretary:
Treasurer: Suzanne Pautler
Membership Chair: Debbie Cutler
Administrative Secretary: Brianna Boes
Member at Large: Frank Montagnino

Well Versed Volunteers:
Managing Editor: Liz Schulte
Editor: Debra Sutton
Editor: Brianna Boes

Appendix C:
Well Versed Sponsors

On behalf of the Columbia Chapter of the Missouri Writers' Guild, we would like to thank everyone who contributed to this year's edition of Well Versed and businesses for their kind support of local authors and the writing community.

Appendix D: Well Versed Judges

Walter Bargen
Scott Dalrymple
Catherine Rankovic
LK Rigel
Lori Younker
Amanda Booloodian
Brianna Boes
Peggy Crawford
Debra Sutton
Karen Mocker Dabson

Made in the USA
San Bernardino, CA
21 May 2016